Through the Eyes of Serenity

Through the Eyes
of Serenity Series, Book One

LEANNA SELLERS

First Paperback Edition: 2019

Paperback ISBN: 978-0-578-88182-9

Library of Congress Control Number: 2019904584

Dedication

To Renee Lindsey Parker and Ingrid Pierson, who helped me stay focused and right on task. Thanks for your patient understanding and support. You encouraged my creativity, and made what might have been a very difficult journey easier and more enjoyable.

Acknowledgements

Many thanks to my editors and friends for the invaluable assistance and untold hours they've devoted to researching ideas, issues, and anecdotes. Also thanks to my friends for the assistance that was given along this journey in completing this book.

Contents

Chapter 1 1

Chapter 2 14

Chapter 3 20

Chapter 4 28

Chapter 5 35

Chapter 6 39

Chapter 7 45

Chapter 8 54

Chapter 9 61

Chapter 10 64

Chapter 11 70

Chapter 12 75

Chapter 13 81

Chapter 14 88

Chapter 15 94

Chapter 16 98

Chapter 17 106

Chapter 18 109

Chapter 19 119

Chapter 20 123

Chapter 21 135

Chapter 22 141

Chapter 23 148

Chapter 24 157

Chapter 25 165

Chapter 26 173

Chapter 27 183

Chapter 28 189

Chapter 29 193

Chapter 30 199

Chapter 31 210

Chapter 32 217

Chapter 1

Bojovník Lake

In the centuries following the nuclear holocaust, lands were scarce to find as the survivors learned to cope with the conditions in the era. In a decade after the twenty first century, a small part of the earth in America was discovered with its beauty untouched by such destruction and was cultivated by families that had come together in those perilous times. In this time, there were battles and rumors of war to fight for what little of the fruitful dirt remained. Their hopes were of bringing peace and healing across the lands. A Russian Militant man named Tomáš who like his father came from a line of brute force family line of warriors, moved to America and met the most beautiful woman he had ever seen named Arabel.

Before the war, two sisters finished high school. Adriena was given the chance to further her education and go to college, because the family could not afford to send both. They had very few places to attend during those perilous times. Serenity sacrificed her own education to let her sister attend. She felt that Adriena would benefit more than she. Adriena became good friends during school with a very handsome boy named Darien. The more she got to know Darien, Adriena felt her twin sister seemed to have more in common. One day while Serenity was singing in the choir. Adriena seemed to notice Darien watching Serenity as if he was captivated by her beauty.

One day she decided to approach him and tell him that Serenity's her sister. A plot started to form in Adriena's mind.

One night their father Tomáš, came in from being on a long trip to see what his next mission would be from his commanding officer. After Serenity fell asleep, Adriena lay in bed hearing her parents' muffled conversation through the thin walls between the bedrooms. "Arabel, listen to me—I have been recalled to active duty on Winter Solstice, unless I am to begin earlier than the first day of winter. Right now, I won't know until it gets closer to time. Please take care of the girls while I am away, and don't let them get into trouble. I will not allow them to date any boys until the turmoil that is coming from the war is over and our family is safe. One day, I hope to explain why to them, but for now, I will not. Should anything happen to me while I'm away, then I would ask you to tell them why."

"Tomáš, you've been through too much. Can't someone else do this? I worry about what war did to you the last time."

"You know, Arabel, I have to do this. I have no choice in this matter, and they promoted me to general. I'll not rest until the one that killed your father is no longer able to force his lies on others, and that goes for all those that follow his cause. I want my family safe from harm and I will do what I must to make that happen."

"Please, I beg of you, don't let this war take my Tomáš away from me. You and the girls are all I have."

Gently, caressing her face with his rough fingertips, he pulled on the sheet to dry her tears and said, "I promise I will try not to let this make me go mad. I love you, and don't you ever forget that! Remember the lake? Those were the best times of my life and I'll never forget. If I don't get the chance to tell them, please tell our girls that I love them and would do anything in the world to keep them safe. I want them to have a better life than we had."

"Tomáš, I wish for you to tell them yourself. I will do as you wish if the time should ever come."

"I promise to do what I can, my love," he said, kissing her deeply. Then they came together as only lovers did to forget the present and the coming parting. They clung close and panted in each others ears, hearts beating as one until they finally drifted into fitful sleep with Arabel's head resting on Tomáš's muscled chest.

The morning dawned early for Arabel. It wasn't quite 4 AM when she cooked a large breakfast for Tomáš. She couldn't stop, even when he protested. He would be gone early again, on the business of war. Who knew when he would be back? As general, Tomáš had many planning and recruiting obligations. Would it be for only a day, a few days, or even weeks? Her heart was troubled as she cleared the now-empty table and got the kitchen ready for a new day with her girls.

It was in the heat of summer and all their chores were done. Serenity and Adriena decided to go to the lake.

"Mom, we have finished our chores and are going to the lake for a swim."

"You girls should pack a lunch, and be careful, not too much sun."

"Thanks, Mom, we've got it covered."

On the way to the lake, Adriena much like her father says, "I wonder if he'll be there? Do you think he'll be there?"

Serenity gave her that look. "Who, Adriena, are you referring to?"

"Darien, of course."

"Perhaps, Adriena. Why?"

"I think you should meet him. He has long been wanting to meet you. It would be great for you to meet. Don't you think?"

"What I think is, it does not matter. He'll never give us the time of day."

"Oh, Serenity, I wish you wouldn't be so negative."

When they arrived, Darien was already there, and had a spot picked out. Then he looked up and watched the girls make their way to another area. Darien's eyes were locked on Serenity.

Her sister just happened to notice. "You know, you should really go talk to him."

"Why me? Why not you?"

"Serenity, I see the way he looks at you. Besides, he fancies you more than me. He watches your every step. I've just seen it."

"I don't know, Adriena. You know Father is recruiting so many, and I'm afraid he might be one of them. Besides, a broken heart is the last thing I need right now."

"Serenity, don't let that get in the way of your happiness. Promise me that you will at least talk to him if he comes over." She gave her that look, and Serenity knew she couldn't say no to it.

Serenity smiled and said, "All right, but only if he comes over."

What she didn't know was that Adriena had talked to him on the last day of school, and he was aware that they would be here. The next thing she knew, he started making his way to where they were.

Adriena whispered in her sister's ear, "Don't look now, but he is coming over. You had better talk to him." Then she smiled at him as if to hide something.

Before Serenity could respond, he was there. Darien bowed to both, holding eye contact with Serenity. "You ladies are looking mighty fine this evening. It's nice to see you again, Adriena. I don't believe I've met your friend here." He reached for her hand and said, "May I?"

Serenity just nodded her head in agreement.

Kissing her hand, he went on, "My name is Darien, and what is your name, if I may ask?"

Adriena gave a wink and said, "I'll leave you to talk. I'm going to mingle with the crowd. Oh, she is actually my sister, Serenity."

While Darien was looking at her, he smiled and nodded his head in approval. Serenity gave Adriena that look that said not to leave her with him. Then she knew her sister had set her up. She couldn't wait to get back home and scold her for it. She started to say something, until Darien moved his eyes back to her.

"You know, your face seems to be a little flushed. Are you okay?"

"Is it? Um, I'm fine, except that I haven't a clue what my sister has said to you. Would you care to enlighten me about the conversation between the two of you? My sister has a bad habit of saying things she shouldn't. And just how do you know my sister?"

"Uh, well... It was when I bumped into her during school a couple of years back, and, well, we have just been talking off and on since then. Nothing out of the ordinary. I noticed she walked with you quite often this past year and asked who you were, and she let me know that you were her sister. I told her then that I would love to meet you someday—soon. Perhaps by the lake, if you go there during the summer. Of course, that was when she said that you would be here after school was out. I guess, by the look on your face, it might not have been the best way to approach you."

"Oh, no, not at all. Thank you for telling me. It's just that my sister can be very straightforward at times."

"My apologies to you. Truth be known, I have wanted to talk to you, or maybe get to know you, for some time now. I've never been able to bring myself to talk to you. Your sister actually helped me with that. It is a pleasure to finally meet you." He bowed to her again as if she were royalty. Although it did run in her family line, she didn't want to be known as royalty.

Serenity blushed at his words. She was blown away by his kindness.

"Would you like to take a walk over to the sandy path along the lake? We can sit and talk over there if you would like."

"Sure, that would be nice," she replied. "Thank you for asking."

They walked over to the beach, and he spread a blanket out for her to sit on. She knew her sister's eyes were watching her.

Adriena smiled at her sister when they made eye contact. Then Serenity continued the conversation on the beach.

Darien looked at her and said, "It sure is beautiful here, do you agree?"

Not saying a word, she just nodded her head, taking in his focused look. What a beautiful warm summer afternoon. The shifting breeze brought with it the scent of cedar from the tall trees in the adjacent forest and the calls of birds taking a shady rest. "You know, your sister was right about one thing."

"And just what would that be?" she said a little sarcastically, fidgeting with her leg, caught off guard.

"Only that your beauty is unlike any other." She gave him a hard look. He stumbled and said, "What I meant was that your beauty is stunning."

"Did she now? My sister said those exact words?"

"Well, um, no, she didn't say that exactly. It is what I say, and I meant no offense or disrespect by it."

With a hint of a smile, she said, "Thank you for the kind words, and no disrespect taken." She felt a little foolish, her face flushed, and she didn't know what to speak into the silence, but then Darien started telling her about his lonely childhood, and how he had always dreamed of a special friend. Seeing her and meeting her through Adriena first had whetted his appetite and driven him into wanting to know her—actually to meet and know her. They were deeply engrossed in conversation for just a bit longer, and then, as the sun started sinking toward the horizon, it was time to go.

"I've enjoyed this time talking with you, but I must take my leave. I need to get my sister and head back home." She began to stand and he jumped up to lend a helping hand.

"Before you go… Would you do me the honor of going out with me, say tomorrow night around five?"

"What, like a date?"

"Yes. Well, no, it doesn't have to be as a date. I would just like to know more about you, if I may ask."

"I don't know…my father is not easy to win over, especially on a date. My father is the general in rank, and he has started recruiting new men to fight the coming war. He is the reason I don't go out much, if at all. Plus, I am afraid he will take away the one thing I would care about if I were to get close to someone. I'm sorry—the more I think about it, the more it doesn't sound like a good idea."

"Hmm, that could be a problem. I would really love to see you again. Could you come to the lake? If you would like, there is a place we can go and no one will bother us, or we can meet again like today. Of course, that is if you would like to see me again. I won't rush anything. You decide."

"Considering how my father is, I think it would be best to come to the lake for now. I can get my sister to agree to this. I really hate sneaking around, but it may be best with the way our father is."

"Then I will see you tomorrow?"

"Yes, I will find a way to be here, but it will be at three, after tea, not at five."

Darien took her hand, looking deep into her eyes. Then he leaned over and kissed it as a gentleman would. His heart was taking little leaps. How lucky he was that this meeting had worked out. He couldn't stop smiling as she walked away. Then he turned and walked up the beach and back to where they had only moments ago spent time talking. How sweet she was. So knowledgeable and yet so innocent. Tomorrow afternoon couldn't arrive soon enough, as far as he was concerned.

Serenity walked up to her sister and her expression showed no emotion for as long as she could hold it.

Adriena couldn't hold back. "Well, how did it go? Please, tell me, Sister."

They got in the horse and buggy. Serenity started off not smiling, trying not to show her sister the bubbles she was feeling inside. But she just couldn't contain it, not with her sister, and with muffled giggles, she let it all flow.

"Adriena, he wants me to meet him back here at the lake tomorrow."

Adriena pulled hard on the reins and the buggy came to an abrupt halt.

"Now, before you say anything, hear me out. First, I don't want him to meet Father yet. You know as well as I what Father will do. So for now, I will be meeting him here at the lake. I need you to help me find a way to come here as much as we can. I know there has to be a way. I think that if anything, with your help we can do this. At least before you go away for the extra schooling. I've never asked for much, or wanted anything more than I do this right now. Can I count on you to help me?"

Adriena, smiling at her, said, "You really like him, don't you?" With that, she clucked her tongue and gave a little snap to the reins, getting the buggy back on a slow roll.

Serenity just couldn't keep from telling her. With her face a little flushed, she said, "Yes, I really do. Such a gentleman. Honestly, he swept me off my feet. We talked and talked. I understand him totally, and it seems like he understands me. We agree on so much and he is funny! He can be such a joker and tease. Don't you dare tell him I said so! Promise, not a word."

Smiling, Adriena said, "I promise, and I would love to come back here anytime you do. I just knew you would like him."

Serenity just smiled, looking at her sister. "Now, how can we keep coming here without raising suspicion? You know Mother catches on quickly if something is out of the ordinary."

"Don't worry, Serenity, we'll think of something."

"I do have one question for you, though. How come you didn't go after him?"

"That's easy, Serenity. I didn't because I knew he fancied you more, the way he asked so many questions about you at all those events we had. I'm so happy that I coaxed Mother into letting me attend."

"Fair enough. And why haven't you told me about any of this until now?"

"To be honest, he asked if we go to the lake, and I told him that we did from time to time, back during those events after school. He said good, then maybe he could meet you. Besides, I know how you are, and you wouldn't have come if I hadn't done it this way, now, would you?"

"I guess you have a point, and I am glad you did."

When they finally arrived home, the sun was starting to dip down low on the horizon. This was Serenity's favorite time of the day. The trees were cast in black **silhouette** against the orange-gold horizon and it always seemed as though the evening was holding its breath and waiting for the last rays of sun to slip away. So peaceful.

The horses were ready to get into the barn, and looked for their hay. The girls went in to wash for dinner. After they ate, their mother asked, "So how was your swim today, and how is it you look dry as a bone?"

Adriena replied, "Mom, we started talking to some of our friends from school that happened to be there, and then decided to soak up some of the rays instead. It was a lovely day for it. We told our friends we will be there again tomorrow."

Their mother looked at them both. With an eyebrow raised, she asked, "Is this to be an everyday occurrence?"

"Mom, it is summertime, and you know I will be off to further my education soon. Besides, I want to spend as much time as I can with my sister before I am sent off to the place we discussed for my schooling." As Adriena replied, she walked with her sister, arm in arm, to sit outside on the porch. It was a beautiful night. The Big Dipper was in full view, and so bright! Not a bit of fog or haze. How immense the starfields were, and how beautiful. Why didn't they do this more often? It made them think of how peaceful things should be and shudder to think of war being so close to their doorsteps.

Their mother, Arabel Kozlov, knew they were close, but couldn't help wondering if there was something else going on. For now, she said to herself, she would let them be. It was too soon to make any judgment call. Their father never said a word, unless they did something he did not approve of.

Adriena called, "Mom, we are going to take a walk and then brush the horses down before turning in."

"Okay, don't stay out too long in the night air. Neither of you need to catch a cold."

"We won't, Mom," they said as they walked away to a quiet place, down to the creek running through their land, that they had used to go to get away from everyone. They sat on a huge moss-covered log on the bank of the creek.

"Serenity, I really hope it works out for you. I so want you to be happy. Enjoy every moment—while you can. I overheard Mom and Dad talking the other night. Dad is being called to fulfill his duty regarding the war."

"Oh no! Adriena, do you know when?"

"They were talking by the end of the summer or on Winter Solstice. It gets worse. He has been told to recruit anyone available to be under his command. We still have the summer, and I intend to enjoy it while I can, and want you to do the same. Don't let this ruin any of your time."

"Adriena, I know what you are saying. I just don't know if I can go through this. I'm going to miss you when you leave, and wish I could go, too. Somebody needs to be here with Mom, and I volunteered. I am the eldest, you know, even if it is only by one hour. Sometimes I wish I had your green eyes, Adriena, and your self-confidence. You are more aggressive than I, and certainly more ambitious, even athletic!" Both girls chuckled, remembering how well Adriena did in archery and gymnastics. "Besides, you can do so much more if you go to school. You also know how to handle Father better than I. I will do the best I can over the summer. I wish Dad was more understanding and not so overbearing. It would make life so much easier for us. Sometimes I feel Mom almost breaking free and then she falls right back in there. Do you feel it?"

Adriana shifted and got more comfortable on the big moss-covered log. "Yes, I do, and I understand what you are saying, too. We are not going to worry about this, are we? We are going to spend as much time as we can at the lake."

"No, I will do my best not to worry about it. I'll tell you a secret. The first time I saw Darien, I fancied him, too. It was when I practiced my choir solo. He happened to be there and stood silently just watching and listening. I even noticed an upturned smile on his lips when I ever so carefully allowed my eyes to just drift over the few onlookers at our last rehearsal. I really hope Father doesn't recruit him."

"Serenity, please don't worry about this now. I want you to promise me that you will enjoy tomorrow, no matter what. Now, it is getting close to bedtime. We need to get to the stables."

"Guess you are right. Let's go," Serenity said with a sigh.

They hurried to the stables, careful not to trip on the stony path to curry and brush the horses. They felt a little guilty about how quickly they dispatched this task and filled water, hay, and oats for these creatures they each loved. They usually spent hours each evening brushing and tending them, with constant chatter about what the next day might bring, or where they might go on their next rides. The patient steeds didn't seem to be bothered by the abbreviated care, and munched happily as the girls left the barn and headed to the house, up the stairs, and to their rooms, waiting for tomorrow to come.

However, it was a while before Serenity would drift off to sleep. She lay on her bed remembering the day, and reliving the countless moments of surprise in getting acquainted with Darien. How his touch aroused her... She knew it shouldn't. The light touches and the butterflies that would begin to quiver, making it hard to concentrate on anything other than their togetherness. Slowly, she moved from the bed to the window. Looking at the stars in the deep blackness of the sky, with just the crowning of a full moon, she started humming a simple tune, adding these words:

Whispers of the Heart

Not a moment passes by
Or a day I don't think of you
Caressing light of your touch
Arousing everything new
If words could tell you
What I am thinking
Let them ring so loudly
Whispering things
Only you can hear
Rousing your thoughts devoutly
Not a moment passes by
In my dreams before my sight
Quivering my very soul
Blissfully within the night
If words could tell you
What I am thinking
Letting them ring so loudly
Whispering things
Only you can hear
Rousing your thoughts devoutly
Not a moment passes by
When I sleep or I'm awake
Imprints felt within your kiss
Tremble my soul, make me quake
If words could tell you
What I am thinking
I'll let them ring so loudly,
Whispering things
Only you should hear

Rousing your heart devoutly
Not a moment passes by
Not a tear within my eye
Nor will I begin to sigh
Nor should I ever deny
Knowing that I need to see
Where we are and need to be
In my heart I decree
Forever, it's you and me
These words will tell you
My heart surrenders
Letting it ring so loudly
I'll whisper things
That you should hear
Arousing your soul devoutly.

As she listened to the beauty of Serenity's song, a smile touched Adriena's lips as her heart felt the specialness of love awakening within her sister. She wondered if she would ever be so lucky as to find or be found by her very own soul mate.

The quiet of the night now crept over the sleeping house, only muffled sounds from the animals in the keep breaking the peaceful silence.

Chapter 2

Hidden Ties

Serenity and Adriena hurriedly got their chores done so they could get ready to enjoy the afternoon at the lake. After feeding the chickens, horses, and their two milk cows, they quickly gathered the eggs needed for the day, and as if they had wings on their feet, they ran to their rooms. Washing up, they quickly changed, then headed to their favorite place to spend as much time as they could there.

"Bye, Mom, we are off to the lake. We will try to be back before dark," they said together.

"Now, you girls know you worry me if it is after dark, so be careful and pack something to eat, just in case you need it."

"Thanks, Mom, we have, and don't worry. We will be fine. We are going to just take our horses this time, without the buggy," Adriena replied.

They got the horses, and on the way to the lake Serenity said, "Do you think Mom is suspicious of anything?"

"No, Serenity, as long as we don't tell her what we are up to and keep it from her as long as we can, we should be fine. I would like to keep it that way as long as possible."

"I know, Adriena. We will just have to do what we can, but she can be very persuasive. Wonder what Darien has in store today?"

Adriena smiled as she said, "Who knows. I wouldn't be surprised if he took you to the place no one goes to for a swim."

"What makes you think that, Adriena? You must know something you're not telling me. Spill it, I need to know."

"Serenity, I just meant he really likes you a lot. All he ever did was talk about you, and I haven't a clue why he hasn't asked you out. At least he finally talked to you. So promise me you will see this one through, and don't cut it off short."

"Fine, but I still think you are hiding something from me."

"Serenity, I promise that is all I know."

Finally making it to the lake, they arrived a little earlier than they anticipated. Adriena noticed Serenity looking around the whole place, smiling as they took their horses to the tie rack. She looked at her sister and said, "Serenity, don't worry, he'll be here. We are a little early, you know."

Looking at Adriena, she said, "I know. Just making sure we didn't overlook him in the crowd, that's all."

"Sure, I believe you," she said coyly while smiling. "Why don't we take our horses to another place? Follow me."

"Where are we going, Adriena?"

"You worry way too much. Don't worry about it. I'm just taking us to another area where it is not crowded, that's all. Now, shall we?"

"Still think you're up to something, and why this area?"

Adriena just smiled at her sister and said, "Me? Up to something? I am only doing what I was asked to do."

"I knew it! Okay, spill it! Who asked you, and why this area? You still haven't told me."

She smiled again. "Now, Serenity, don't get all worked up over nothing… Darien asked me to get you to come here. He did not tell me why. Honestly, that's all I know."

Serenity gave her a look as if she was still questioning her. "Just when did you find the time to talk to him?"

"To be honest, he said this before we left school the last day. Quit worrying about it and just go with it. Besides, you really like him, so don't you dare blow it, Serenity."

"Okay, fair enough. Just amazes me that you did all this with his help. What I would like to know is how in the world you pulled this off," she said with a smile as they tied off the horses.

Adriena made a motion with her hand like she was zipping her lips. "Sorry, Sis, can't disclose all my secrets."

Giggles overcame both girls as Darien came up behind them and said, "And just what is so funny?"

Startled, Serenity retaliated with a reply, while giving her sister that look. "Oh, just my sister being herself."

"I'm going to mingle with some friends in the crowd. You guys have fun. Don't do anything I wouldn't do." She winked at Serenity to express her meaning and walked back the way they had come.

Serenity's blood pressure had risen, and being a little flustered in her expression didn't help matters. She turned to Darien and managed a halfhearted smile.

Looking at Serenity, he said, easing the tension in the air, "Don't worry about your sister. I promise there is no ulterior motive."

Serenity looked at him with a devious smile and said, "I wouldn't put it past my sister."

"Come on, let's go. I have prepared a special picnic for us. Perhaps we can sit and talk for a while. I'd like to get to know you better."

She looked at him and replied, "As much as my sister has apparently talked to you, I would wager you know more about me than I do you. Thanks to my sister, of course."

"On the contrary, I don't know as much as you think I do. I swear it."

"Okay, I believe you."

They sat and talked for hours, and then went for a swim. Being a little coy, he splashed her face when she least expected it. With a scarlet face, she began her retaliation and splashed back at him. With each splash getting harder, he moved closer to counter them by embracing her in his arms. A little startled now, her eyes fixed on his, she wondered what was coming next. Leaning closer, just inches from her face, reading her eyes, he chanced a kiss. Almost melting in his arms, she realized there really was no one around and started pulling away.

A little confused, he looked at her and said, "Did I do something wrong? I do apologize for being a little straightforward."

"No, it isn't you. It's me," she said.

Holding her gaze with concern, he replied, "Please, tell me what's wrong."

"Nothing is wrong, Darien. I'm just more worried about what may happen by Winter Solstice."

"Can you tell me? I might be able to ease your worry."

"Honestly, I don't think you can help, but I will tell you. You see, my father is a ruthless general in the Neachean Force that has been called to serve again."

Cutting in, he said, "That's not so bad."

"Darien, it gets worse. He is also recruiting new and freshly graduated high school students. I am worried that he will recruit you. This is why I don't get close to anyone." He listened as she continued. "My father is a bit temperamental and holds nothing back. He always ruins what I have as soon as he knows I am very happy, and for me, that is hard to hide."

Throwing his arms around her, he said, "Don't worry, I will do everything I can to keep that from happening. You have my word on that." Lifting her chin to his, he said, "Now, where were we?" With a hint of a smile from Serenity, he kissed her again.

As she rested in his arms, they lost all track of time. It was as if time were standing still as the light around them started to both fade and glow in the backdrop of a beautiful sunset. Looking deeply into her eyes, he kissed her again.

With perfect timing, Adriena came up, clearing her throat. Quickly, they pulled apart as if they had been caught. Looking at her sister, Serenity asked, "Um, how long have you been there?"

"Only a few minutes. Just wanted to remind you it is getting late, and we don't want to worry Mom."

Giving Adriena that look as if to say how rude of you to interrupt, she replied, "I guess you're right. I'm sorry, Darien, we cannot stay. We must get back to keep from raising any concerns." Then she looked at her sister as a hint for her to leave. "I'll be along in a minute." Adriena was trying to hide the smile that she could not contain, while Serenity had so many thoughts running through her head.

Darien jumped to his feet and lent a hand to help her up, which she gladly accepted. He pulled her close, kissing her lips one last time, and asked, "When will I see you again?"

"Darien, I will do my best to be here tomorrow. We will find a way."

The next day, Serenity and Adriena rushed getting the chores around the house finished. Her mom said, "Shouldn't you girls stay home today? It looks like rain is coming."

"Oh, Mom," Adriena replied. "We will be okay, and we'll take the carriage just in case. Besides, if we get caught in it, we have a friend from school who lives nearby and has told us if ever the need arises, we can stay there. We promise to be careful, and you need not worry."

"And just who is this friend of yours?"

"You remember Alysa Mytear, don't you? She helped us with our studies when we needed it, as did we for her," Adriena replied.

"Yes, I remember. Okay, I'll allow it, as long as you don't come down sick. You girls be careful now." Giving them that look, she said, "Both of you. I mean it."

"Yes, Mom. We will. You need not worry," they both replied.

Chapter 3

Cryptic Notion

Finally they were off to the lake. Adriena looked at Serenity and said, "Serenity, I'm going to see Alysa and talk to her while you are with Darien. I'm sure you won't mind, will you?" she said with a devious smile. Serenity looked at her sister and said, "I still think you planned all of this."

Adriena replied, "I'll never tell."

She knew her sister was up to something, but she didn't really care. Darien had won her over with very little effort.

Finally they made it, and sat gracefully, waiting for Darien.

"Adriena, do you think he knows where we'll be?"

She smiled as she looked at her sister and then looked up. "Of course, why don't you turn around and see for yourself."

Serenity turned around with her face flushed scarlet. Looking up, she managed a weak smile and shyly said, "Hello."

Extending his hand, he said, "Shall we?" Then he looked at Adriena to say with a smile, "You don't mind if I steal her away, do you?"

Adriena replied, "No, not at all. I was just leaving to go to our friend's house. Serenity, you know where I'll be if you need me," she said, smiling as she walked away.

Looking at Serenity, he said, "Want to go for a swim before the rains move in?" As if she could resist and say no.

"Sure." He took her hand, leading her to the water over slippery stones and through some blooming cattails.

Stepping in slowly, she said, "Definitely going to rain."

"How do you know?"

"For one, this water has a chill, and it's always chilly before the rain or first snow."

"Well, come a bit closer, I'm sure it can heat up a bit," he said as he pulled her close enough to touch his skin.

Not resisting his moves, she said, "We shouldn't be here"––as he lightly caressed her lips with his––"alone."

"Why not? There's no one here. Besides, you've already stolen my heart, and I don't want to be apart from you," he said as he looked deeply into her eyes. He moved in closer and kissed her. With a sigh, she just relaxed into his strong arms.

Just as things were heating up, rains descended. Quickly, they moved out of the water, grabbed their things, and ran to an enclosed gazebo with a fireplace in the center.

Looking at Serenity, he said, "Are you cold?"

With her teeth chattering, she replied weakly, "Just a…a b-b-b-bit."

He quickly lit the fireplace and displayed a little picnic. "Would you care for a bite to eat?" She had been fine until he mentioned the word eat, and her stomach let her know it. Embarrassed by the little growl her stomach made, she could only manage a nod yes. There were blueberries, strawberries, apples, oranges, and grapes from the vineyard nearby. "I picked these for you. Maybe a little wine to go with it, if you like. Of course, I do have some water if you'd prefer."

"A little wine will be fine. My father gives us some on special occasions. When did you have time to do all of this?"

Smiling at her, he replied, "I got here about an hour before you showed up."

"I see, and you just happened to have some firewood on hand for this as well?"

"Honestly, this was already here, but I was told if it was needed, I could use it."

"Wait a minute. You know the owners of this place?"

"Of course, didn't your sister tell you?"

"My sister! Humph! Apparently she has a habit of not telling me everything."

"My apologies, I thought for sure she would have told you."

"No, no, it's okay, but I will be having a nice little talk with her. So who owns this place?"

"My father does. He will pass it to me when he is gone. He made sure to put it in his will."

Surprised, she said, "Wow! Your father owns this? You're kidding, right?"

"No, it is all true. I would love for you to meet him someday. Maybe before the summer is over, perhaps?"

"That would be nice. I would love to meet your father. But not right now, of course."

"It will be up to you. I'm very patient. Here, try one of these strawberries," he said, pulling her down next to him.

She let out a little laugh while he poured the wine. Then he fed her the strawberry. She ate it slowly, savoring every bite, with a little juice running down her chin. He took his thumb and lightly removed it while holding her gaze. Moving closer, he kissed her again.

In Serenity's mind, she said to herself, "My sister knows better than to leave me alone with him." Then she had another thought: "Then again, was this her plan all along?" Pushing the thought out of her mind, she just enjoyed the moment. Kissing him back feverishly, she was about to lose control. She pulled back reluctantly and looked him in the eyes while biting down on her lip.

Looking at her, he said, "Is there something wrong?"

"We shouldn't be here. I mean, I shouldn't feel this way, but I feel like I have known you a long time, yet we've only just met."

Raking his fingers across her lips as if to shush her, he replied, "If it means anything, I feel the same way. We can take it slow or let our hearts guide us. I'll go as fast or slow as you like."

"Honestly, part of me doesn't want this to end," she said.

"And the other part? What does it say?" he asked.

"Darien, my heart says don't stop." With a hint of a smile on her face, Serenity closed her eyes. Leaning into him, she kissed him back. Things began to radiate between them. He slid her strap off her shoulder, leaving it bare, while kissing and softly caressing her skin. Moving to the other side, he began to remove the other one. Just as he moved in to kiss it, someone knocked on the door.

Moving hurriedly, he said, "Quickly, grab your things and hide behind the door of the bathroom. I will let you know when it is clear."

Doing exactly what he said, Serenity stepped back and melted into the shadows. He opened the door, only to find it was Adriena. She looked at him and said, "Have you seen my sister?"

He said, "It's okay, Serenity. It's just your sister." Serenity came out and saw her sister standing there.

"I'm sorry to intrude on you, but I got word our father is headed this way looking for us. If we hurry, we can meet him on the path on the way home."

"I'm sorry, Darien, but I must go. I will try to get word to you when we can come back."

He pulled her close and kissed her, not wanting to leave. Adriena grabbed her by the arm and said, "Now! We must hurry if you guys want to see each other again."

Serenity looked at him with a saddened heart, and in a whisper, she said, "I'm really sorry, but I must go."

Racing to their carriage, quickly putting their things in, Adriena urged the horses to move. Looking back, Serenity saw Darien still standing in the doorway, shirtless. Another memory of him imprinted in her mind, bringing a smile to her face instantly. All the while, her twin sister, who noticed her expression, felt in her own heart the wondrous feelings of love that emanated from Serenity.

"Looks like you two had quite a time." With a smile on her face, Adriena said, "I shudder at the thought of what would have happened if I had not shown up when I did. So do tell, I want to hear."

Being coy, Serenity looked at Adriena and said, "I'll never tell."

Adriena looked at her and said, "No matter, the look on your face tells me enough, and don't forget, twins share feelings, even when they don't intend to."

Serenity smiled at the memory. "All I can say, Adriena, is I am glad you showed up when you did. I don't think I could have resisted if I had wanted to."

Adriena smiled at her sister. "From the looks of it, sounds like you had a nice time. Please tell me you didn't."

"No, but if you hadn't shown up when you did, we would've. I know this is crazy, and we've not known each other long, but my heart is racing every time I'm around him. I don't want to lose him or what we have."

Adriena looked at her sister. "I'm no expert, but it sounds like you are in love, Sister. I've known since I first met Darien that you were the one. I felt it as sure as if he had longed for me."

Serenity looked at her sister and said, "Perhaps it's true. I know one thing––I don't want this to end."

She smiled back at Adriena. Then they looked up to see their father coming closer to them.

"Adriena, I sure hope Father isn't furious with us."

"I agree, Serenity."

Their father stopped to say, "Are you girls okay? Your mother and I have been so worried about you."

"Father, we are fine, you didn't have to come and check on us."

"Actually, I was on my way to the Bonnaires', because I need to talk to his son. I was hoping I'd run into the both of you so I could let your mother know that you are both fine. Now I guess you will save me the trouble."

Adriena replied, "What on earth do you need to talk to his son about, if I may ask?"

"Now, that's none of your concern, so you need not worry. It's not as if you know him anyway, now, do you?"

"Father, I do know him. He is a good friend of mine from school. We had some classes together."

"It will be okay, as long as he is a friend and nothing more. I trust I don't have to worry about that, now, do I?"

"No, Father, as you wish. He is only a friend. To say for the sake of argument, what if I were to date him—of course, not that I would?"

"First of all, Adriena, I forbid it. Second of all, we will have no more discussion about it. Am I clear on this?"

"Yes, Father, very clear, but I can still remain friends with him, can I not? Would you begrudge my friendship?"

"Adriena, I will allow friendship only, nothing more. Understood?"

"Yes, Father, I will do as you ask."

"Understand, Adriena, times are not good right now. I want to keep you girls safe and unharmed. War is upon us, and I don't want you mixed up in it in any way. I'm sure your mother has told you I have been called back to duty to serve as the commander of the Neachean Force in the fall before winter's first drift. Now, I don't want you girls to worry. I will do everything I can to keep you safe."

25

"Father, I heard you were recruiting. Please, don't recruit my friend, I beg of you."

"Now, Adriena, that is not your concern, or your business, for that matter. I have no control over it. I suggest you enjoy what time you have. It will be best for everyone involved. Now, enough discussion. I don't want to hear any more about it. Are we clear? Do not force my hand on this. Understood?"

"Yes, Father. I'll not say another word."

Then her father said, "What about you, Serenity? Do you have any friends I should know about?"

Doing her best to hold her composure, careful not to let him see through her, Serenity replied, "No, Father, just Alysa Mytear."

"Very well. You girls head on home to keep your mom from worrying. Tell her I won't be back until really late tomorrow, or perhaps not until the day after. There is so much brewing right now. No telling where it will end, or when it will spill over into a full-blown war."

"Yes, Father," they said together.

Just as soon as he left, Adriena stopped a little ways up the path. She looked at her sister and said, "Don't worry, we will think of something. We're not going to let him and this horrible war ruin things now. Besides, there is always a way around his shenanigans." Her green eyes twinkled with her mischievous smile.

"We can do this together. If I know Darien, he will find a way, come hell or high water."

"Adriena, do you really believe that? How will we find a way come winter?"

"Serenity, let's not think about that now. Just worry about the here and now, one step at a time. Now, dry those tears up before we go home, shall we?"

"I guess you're right. I wonder why he fancies me more than you. And why haven't you pursued him?"

"Honestly, I think of him as a friend. To tell you the truth, all he has ever done is talk about you, and how he wanted to meet you. I just decided to arrange it, and I would not ever change it. Besides, from the way he looks at you, I'd say he's in love with you, too. You should enjoy every moment you can spend with him."

Adriena's words brought a smile to Serenity's face. She said, "You're right, Adriena. Thanks for cheering me up. I will do everything I can. Now, what about Mom? She can read us both like a book."

Chapter 4

Perceptions

"Don't worry, I think we can elude Mother for now. It will be a matter of how long we can keep it up. Eventually, we may have to tell her."

"That is true, Adriena, then we would have to pray she doesn't tell Father. I really don't think she can hide it from him that long."

"We'll just cross that bridge should the need arise. Now, what can we come up with for going to the lake again?" Adriena said to her sister. "Why do you think I went to see our friend?" she said with a smile.

"And just what do you have in mind, as if I didn't already know?"

Adriena replied, "Let's just say we are going to have a sleepover. Hope that is okay with you. Her mom knows how Father is, and will do anything so we can have some fun."

Smiling, Serenity said, "Fun indeed. You think of everything, don't you?"

"Well, somebody has to, don't you think?" she said with a devious grin. "Now, I'll let Mother know we're back, and then we can take care of the horses. By the way, you need to hide that glow from Mother or she will home in on it."

"Guess you're right. I'll do my best and work on it," she said.

"Hey, Mom," Adriena said. "We unhitched the horses and got them settled. We're going to wash up for dinner and then finish taking care of the them."

"That's fine, dear. I would like to talk to you girls while your father is away with official business that he is to attend to till tomorrow."

"Yes, Mother," they replied. While washing up, Serenity said, "I wonder what this could be?"

"I haven't a clue. We need to not reveal a thing, at least until we know what's going on."

"Adriena, you're so much better at this than I. I sure hope I can do this."

"You can, Serenity." In a whisper she said, "Just think of how much you want to be with him. I guarantee you will do almost anything to make that happen."

"Okay, I hope you're right. I will do my best."

"Oh, and we are staying the night at Alysa's tomorrow to enjoy the cookout. Maybe two weeks if we can persuade Mother."

"That sounds divine." Serenity replied with a devious smile.

Mother walked in right as Serenity said that. "And just what sounds divine?"

Adriena said, "Oh, Mother, we will discuss it after dinner, if that's okay."

"That's fine, dear. You girls are getting very mischievous here of late. I hope you don't upset your father. He has been very tolerant lately, but that may change soon."

"What do you mean, Mother? We've done nothing wrong."

"As I said, we will talk after dinner. Now, are you girls ready to eat?"

"We're starving," Adriena replied.

"Speak for yourself," Serenity said. "I'm not that hungry."

"Oh, and just why not?" Mother asked.

"I just meant I had some fruit not long ago, but I can eat a little something. I meant no disrespect."

"Okay, dear. Fair enough. Where did you find the fruit?"

"We just picked some wild strawberries, two oranges, and apples along the way back."

"Aren't those oranges and apples on the Bonnaires' land?"

"Yes, Mother, but we were given permission anytime we would like some. Darien said we could before school was out," Adriena replied.

Feeling butterflies in the pit of her stomach at the sound of his name, Serenity feared her Mother could see right through her.

Serenity cleared her throat to say, "What are we having for dinner? It smells very good."

"Venison that your father brought back yesterday and cleaned to be prepared for tonight, some cornbread, greens, corn, and some strawberry pie for dessert."

In a bit of shock, Serenity asked, "Where did you find the strawberries around here?"

"I didn't. I gathered them from a little ways up the road. Why, dear? Is there something wrong?"

Stumbling over her words a little, she said, "No, Mother, I bet they will be good." She tried a weak smile as she changed the subject, while knowing those strawberries were close to where she and Darien swam in the lake. Now she had an uneasy feeling about this.

Adriena noticed right off something was wrong. She knew she would have to be very careful around this. Mother had an uncanny way of finding things out. She just hoped their mother would not say a word to their father.

They sat down at the table for dinner. Mother said, "Let's eat, shall we?"

"Wow! Mother, this tastes divine."

"Glad you like it, Adriena."

"I agree, Mother, this is very good."

"Why, thank you, Serenity. When you ladies get finished, I would like us to sit for a bit and have a little talk, woman to woman. Just to ease the tone and your thoughts, this will only be between us. I will not tell Father unless it is absolutely necessary. Okay, girls, let's finish our meal."

Sitting on pins and needles, wondering what this was all about, Serenity was trying to push it from her mind. Adriena noticed the tension and wished she could calm her nerves.

Serenity said, "I can't eat another bite. Will you please excuse me? I'd like to go wash up, and I'll put my plate in the sink."

"Okay, dear, but you've hardly touched your food."

"I'm sorry, Mother, I must have eaten too many fruits. I'm just not very hungry," Serenity replied.

"Me too, Mother. May we be excused?"

"All right, you girls, hurry back so we can have our discussion. I will wash the dishes until you return."

"Yes, Mother. May we finish taking care of the horses, and then have this discussion? We need to get them brushed down and fed."

"Okay, you may go ahead and do that first. Then we will have our little talk."

Adriena replied, "Thanks, Mother. We will hurry and then wash up."

They walked outside to where the horses were. Unhitching the first mare, Adriena worried about her sister, and she didn't say a word until they were out of their mother's sight and pulling the horses into the barn.

"Adriena, Mother knows about Darien."

"You don't know that for sure."

"Yes, I do. Those strawberries she picked were right where we went swimming. I know she had to have seen us."

"Serenity, don't jump to that conclusion yet. Let's just hear what Mother says first. Then, if she does, we will have no choice but to tell her. I don't think she will say a word to Father. It will be okay."

"I hope you are right. If there is anything I've wanted in my entire life, it is him. I will be devastated without him." Serenity mulled over this possibility as she curried her mare down and settled her in the stall.

"Don't you worry about this. We will find a way. I promise there is a way to get around them. We will just have to be more aware.

There is one way that will work, but I don't want to do that unless we have no choice. For now, don't worry about it, okay? Promise me." Then she poured the oats into the horses' feeders while Serenity put the harnesses on the pegs.

"What way, Adriena? Please, tell me."

She looked to see if Mother was still in the kitchen. Yes, the figure in the window was still washing up the dishes. "Look, Serenity, if we have to, I would do this in a heartbeat, and would not hesitate in doing so. I can make arrangements so that you can see Darien without me coming along."

"No, Adriena, I don't want that to happen."

"Serenity, if this is the only choice, somebody could stay here so that we can keep an eye on what they do, and I would gladly do it. Besides, I want to see you happy, and you deserve it. He is worth this small effort, don't you think?"

"Yes, but what about you?"

"Serenity, don't worry about me. I still have to go to school, and I have nothing to lose. You have a lot to gain from this. I know you would do this for me, and I am doing this for you. Love you, Sis, and you deserve this happiness no matter what, okay?"

"Are you sure about this? I can't believe this is already happening, and we haven't even gotten into summer long enough."

"Yes, I'm sure. Now, we need to get the carriage put away quickly and get back to Mother before she comes out here and gets us," she said. They both laughed as they hurried with their task.

Linking arms, they walked back to the house, ran upstairs to wash up, and then went back to the sitting room to talk.

Mother looked at the girls, and noticed how difficult this was for them. "Look, girls, I know one or both of you would like to go out with a gentleman. The reason your father does not want to allow it is because of the war we are facing. It is getting closer to us, and we want to keep you both as safe as possible. He has tolerated you going to the lake, mainly because of who it belongs to, and they are very good people. I can tell by the look on your faces that one of you is in love. There are many things that give that away, and I have gone through it myself. So I know, and there is nothing wrong with it, except for the timing. Your father would not tolerate it at all, but I can't sit by and let you be unhappy, especially for the summer. For this reason, I did get him to allow this. I will warn you to be very careful in how you proceed, because your Father is not as forgiving as I am. Now, Serenity, please tell me who it is. I am aware of your meeting, and I believe you are smart enough to know this, am I right? Before you say a word, I will not tell your father as long as you don't violate his wishes. Is this clear?"

"Yes, Mother. It is Darien, and I fear that Father is trying to recruit him to serve in that stupid war," she said, standing up as if to leave.

"Serenity, sit back down, please, and let me finish." Serenity sat back down, silently. "All I'm saying is, do not let your father see you with him. He is very defensive of you both. I know he can be cruel, but I really believe he means well."

"Why does Father have to be so overprotective? Doesn't he know he is suffocating us just to move about? Mother, I don't want to lose Darien. Not now. I can't bear it. Please."

"My, you have really fallen for this young man, haven't you?"

"Yes, Mother. I do love him. There, I said it. Now what happens?"

"We will keep this between us. I promise not to say a word to your father. Hopefully you won't worry about this. You must use caution if you see him. You know your father, and he will put a halt to it very quickly. This will ruin any chance you could have had with Darien if this happens. Do you understand?"

"Yes, Mother. I just wish we could have a normal life like our friends, without any worries or fears."

Adriena spoke up, saying, "Speaking of friends, Mother, Alysa invited both of us to their cookout, and they will be having fun and games during this time. She asked if we could stay two or three weeks. Can we stay so we can help with these festivities, please? It will give us a chance to know them better. She and her parents asked us to come, and we don't want to ruin any friendships we have."

"I see, and will there be any boys invited to this, Adriena?"

"No, ma'am, she said it will be just us girls. Can we? Please?"

"Okay, I will allow it this time. I will have to figure out something to tell your father. You know he was raised very different from us, so it can be difficult to get him to understand. Just go and enjoy yourselves. I will do what I can, okay?"

Both girls hugged their mother. Adriena replied, "Thank you, Mom. May we be dismissed?"

"Yes, you may, and rest well. Tomorrow, don't worry about anything around here. I will take care of it so you can go and enjoy your time with your friends."

After hugging their mother, they ran upstairs and attempted to sleep through all the excitement.

Just as Serenity drifted off to sleep, Darien quietly came up to to the window. Thinking to himself, "I hope Serenity is awake so I can tell her of my plans tomorrow hoping she will agree." As luck would have it Adriena is awake, so I must rely on her to help me keep a secret and surprise her sister. Adriena heard a little ping on the window, as she took a look to see what it is, she noticed Darien.

Darien got flustered seeing that it is her sister Adriena. Quickly changing his thoughts he decided to make it a secret and needs Adriena to help him surprise Serenity. As Darien was leaving his thoughts went back to what he was planning hoping Serenity would go along. He reminisced of the time they shared, hoping she would respond to his longing for her, knowing she will be his first and only.

Chapter 5

Clandestine place

The next day, the girls got up very early, packing what they needed for this trip. "Should we pack two or three dresses and a fancy dress for the dance, Adriena? What about a pair of hiking pants and shirts?" Facing the reality of being away for three weeks on their own, they found holding their composure to hide their true excitement was not easy.

"Serenity, Mother would be in a fit if she knew what I was doing. I'm not even going to mention anything about Father. So don't you reveal anything, and you need to hide this well."

"What are you talking about, Adriena?"

"It will not be only we girls' company. What you don't know is Darien will be out there. I will take you to where he said to meet him. He has plans that I don't know. The only thing he told me was where to meet him, nothing else."

Serenity's butterflies surfaced again at his name. Giving her sister that look as if she were up to something yet again, she said, "How in the world do you know this?"

"Because, Sister, he was outside our window after Mother was asleep. He climbed the trellis to tell me while you were asleep."

"He was here and you didn't wake me?"

"Truthfully, I was going to, but he asked me not to. He had to tell me and hurry back before he was caught even leaving his own land.

Besides, he wants to surprise you," she said while giving Serenity that devious grin.

"I can't believe it. My own sister's keeping secrets from me." Returning the smile the same way she received it, she said, "At least I have a few of my own, too, and I won't tell this one, or maybe I can tell you some of it."

"Do tell me, Sister, you know I'll not say a word."

"What Mother knew, I caught a glimpse of right before we ran to the gazebo. I was afraid of what she might say, and with good reason of what she may still."

"Why didn't you tell me?

"Honestly, I wasn't quite sure until she talked to us. I feared what she might have said. I am glad you did not tell her where we would be this time. I'd like to keep it that way, if possible. Can I count on you for this?"

"You know you can, Sis. Not a word."

They finally made it to Alysa's house. After staying the night, before their journey ahead, they prepared for everything that was needed. After breakfast, they hurried on their way to where things were already set up to stay. When they stopped, Adriena took Serenity to her destiny. Serenity's heart raced at the sight of him. He took her by the hand, looking at Adriena. "We will meet back here in about a week, unless anything unforeseen changes. Enjoy your time while you can."

Adriena turned to Darien and said, as she poked him in his chest lightly, "Now, you take good care of my sister, you hear?"

Darien smiled and replied, "Now, Adriena, you know I will do just that, and no harm will come to her. I give you my word on it," he said, looking at Serenity.

As the two departed with their own belongings, Serenity's butterflies had risen, affecting her voice as she tried to speak through it.

Adriena returned to the camp with Alysa.

"Where's your sister? Isn't she joining us?" Alysa asked.

"No, it will just be us for the week or so. She has more important plans to fulfill. I'll not go into detail, so can we leave it at that?"

"She shouldn't be alone out here."

"I assure you, she is not alone. Please, don't ask. Besides, she will return and will be well taken care of. Why don't we enjoy this time? We can tell stories, go fishing, if you like. Is there anyone you fancy?"

"There was one. Unfortunately, he was recruited to fight in the Neachean War that your father now leads. I wanted the opportunity for a chance to know him better. Now there is no way for that to happen. So now I just try to look forward to going to college."

"Really? I, too, am going to college. Where will you be attending?"

"I'm to attend Cambridge University in the fall. An all-girls academy with an all-guys not too far from it. They hold dances adjoining the schools together."

"How interesting is that? I am attending the same as you. Maybe we can room together."

"Oh, wow! Now I don't feel so alone attending. I wonder if we can get our parents to take us together. I heard this school can arrange it if the parents ask and agree to this."

"That would be splendid. Do you have an idea what your study will be?"

"Yes, Alysa, I'm to become a nurse, in hopes to help heal those in my father's war. I want peace."

"How interesting. I'm to study in the medical field, too. What better way to heal our men, if we ever find any."

As laughter broke out between them, Adriena said, "We need to get our things settled if we are to be here a week or so. I'm thankful we have food in that cabin."

"I agree. Are you worried about your sister at all?"

"No, I know she's in good hands. She will be fine. We learned a lot from our father about how to survive, if the need should ever arise. Please, make sure that if anyone asks, she was with us, okay?"

With a look of confusion, Alysa agreed. "What would happen if, for any reason, they found out she wasn't?"

"Let me see if I can explain. It is because of our father and who he is. Our father was not born of these lands. He is from across the deep blue. His family came to our lands due to the war that broke out, causing them to flee from what they'd known. He was sixteen years of age at that time. He earned his title as a commander for being ruthless against his enemies. Mother said he's gotten worse over the years, and every time war breaks out, it makes him even worse. He is very strict and keeps a very close eye on us. This is why we are not able to enjoy what you call normal. I don't tell you about my sister now because our father has a way of finding things out without us knowing how. If I don't tell you something, this is why. The less we know, the better we will be. I hope this answer to your question is sufficient."

"Quite sufficient, and thank you for telling me. I understand more."

They gathered everything needed to get settled. Then they decided to go by the nearby stream and enjoy the coolness of the water. Adriena's thoughts began to wander, thinking about her sister and how her hike was going.

Chapter 6

Forbidden Mist

"Darien, where are we going?" There was a comforting breeze blowing through a narrow pass in the trail ahead. He took her hand, leading her through a rocky path, and said, "To a place no one knows exists, except for me, my father, and now you. Watch your step, and don't worry, we're almost there. Do you need to stop for a little bit?"

"No, I'm fine, let's continue," she said with just a hint of concern, looking at the rocky path ahead.

Seeing it in her face, he replied, "Don't worry, I'll guide you through. I believe you will love what you see." Then they walked through what looked to be a hidden entrance. Trees, green shrubbery, and rocks. He moved a big rock that appeared to be part of a much larger slide of rocks now permanent to the landscape. They entered quickly, closing it right behind them.

He looked at her and said, "I was exploring through these parts when I was young, after the war my father went through. Not long after, my mother was stricken by some type of fever, and things took a turn for the worse. We worked feverishly to find a cure, but to this day, we don't know what caused it. It wasn't long after that I stumbled across this area. I could tell it had never been touched when I found it. Being as young as I was, and curious, I began to explore as much as I could. Now, follow closely and watch your step." He smiled at her, never letting go of her hand as they continued through the rather narrow opening.

"Wow, no wonder you know this area. How is it no one knows anything about this, and how did you find it?"

"To tell you the truth, Serenity, I was going to climb that rock and it moved. When I opened it, I walked in to see where it led. What I found intrigued my curiosity. I explored to find out where it might go and to see if it would give my family a safe haven if we needed it, in case war broke out again."

They came into a huge chamber. As they stepped through, the view took her breath away! Sparkling jewels lit up the chasm of what seemed to be forbidden pools, with a waterfall's mist cascading down lichen, and moss covered the rock walls. There were ferns interspersed with late-blooming lilies that caught the sun's rays shining from hundreds of feet above in what appeared to be a crater hole. Looking at the amazement on her face, Darien nudged her forward.

"Here we are. A place set up for us. I laced it with rose petals to enhance the fragrance and color of this place, pillows, quilts, a soft mattress for comfort. However, this does not hold a candle to your beauty," he said as he kissed her hand. "Hope you don't mind, I set up two areas, one for you and one for me, to make you feel more comfortable, if you like."

She gave him that look, as if he knew exactly what it meant. "My, those pools look so inviting. Do you know how the water is? Perhaps the temperature? It's starting to feel a bit warm in here." She unbuttoned a couple of buttons at the top of her blouse and said, "Or maybe it's just me." There was no mistaking the look she gave.

He looked at her with a smile and said, after he kissed her, "Let's unpack our belongings. Perhaps a bite to eat and something to drink, if you like, before we enter, shall we? I can't explain how this can be, but the temperature is like this all year round, even when the temperatures drastically plummet outside and snow lies feet deep. Perfect, if you ask me."

"Really? That sounds delightfully heavenly," she said, overtaken by the beauty surrounding them. She looked at the waterfall cascading into the pool. The natural light the cavern gave was just stunning to see. She couldn't utter another word at the sight.

Looking at her and the expression on her face, he replied, "I know how you feel. I felt the same as you when I first found it, and I can think of no one better to share this with than you." Softly, with a light caress of his lips across her brow, he said, "This will be only for us to see, and I want to keep it that way. Maybe one day, perhaps when everything settles down and there is no more war, we can possibly share this with our family. As you can see, this is hidden very well. I will see that it stays that way. I can promise you that. Would you like something to eat before we go for a swim?"

"Sure, I am a little famished."

Her stomach began to make a sound. He replied, "Sounds like more than a little," and laughed.

Embarrassed, she just laughed along with him. "What about my sister? Can we at least tell her?"

"For now, let's not, but I promise to tell her when the time is right. Okay?"

"I guess you're right. Just hate to keep things from her."

"No offense, but from what I've seen, she has done well keeping things from you," he said with a hint of a smile.

"I suppose you're right about that. Now, what do we have to eat?" she said as her stomach was making more sounds.

"Let's see, I have some dried venison, different kinds of fruits, freshly baked bread, some roasted potatoes, and these long green slender crisps that I can't recall the name of, but they are very tasty."

"Wow! When did you find the time to do all of this?"

"Well now, I can't disclose all my secrets, can I?" Both laughed at his reply, and then they ate.

She leaned into his arms, and they rested a bit from the long hike to get there.

Serenity changed into the two-piece swimsuit she'd made and was forbidden to wear in public. The soft fabric clung to her, caressing every curve, highlighting her complexion, and enhancing her stunning beauty. She came out, looking deeply at him, and a look of desire crossed his face. Stunned at her form, his eyes never leaving hers, Darien was rendered speechless. She said coyly, "You know, you can say something."

"Mon amour Tu es belle!"

Aroused by his language while his gaze penetrated her soul, she replied, "Tell me what you just spoke, and what language is that? I only know my father's language and that of these lands."

He lightly caressed her face, holding her gaze steady. "It means, "My love, you are ravishing!" Then he said, "Come this way. I'll show you the forbidden pools." Serenity stepped into the waist-deep water, which was surprisingly, yet comfortably, cool. Slowly, he pulled her close in front of him while holding her with a penetrating gaze, piercing right through to her very soul.

There was no way out of this, nor at the moment did she care. "Nemůžu uvěřit, že se to děje tak rychle. Jen dech," she said in her language. "Can't believe this is happening so fast. Must breathe."

He caressed her lips lightly with his fingertips, a fever welling up inside from her astounding beauty. Enticed by her white-lace swimsuit that enhanced every curve, he replied, "Ah, but it is, my love, it is." He was just barely inches from her face, now lightly brushing her lips with his. Trembling with weakness from deep within, she gave in to the waves of seduction that enveloped her.

What control she had was no longer there. Under the waterfall's mist, they were surrounded by cascading light. Now pressing more firmly, he deepened his kiss while his taut muscles rippled and the initially warm embrace became a need for so much more. She gave in willingly, as there was no other place she'd rather be. He lifted her slightly out of the water, while she wrapped her legs around his waist, and he caressed her every inch. Stopping for just a bit, she gazed into his eyes of green. He said, "Serenity, I won't unless you are sure." They were surrounded by cascading waterfalls, which fell into the pools within the cavern, which had smooth limestone and marbled floors that looked to be carved into perfection.

"Darien, you must know my father has kept a chain on us, and everything we have ever loved has been stripped from us before we could enjoy our experience. For once, my father has no control, and I will not let him take my happiness away from me. My sister knows this very well, and she knows my heart. So when you ask if I am sure, my answer is, indubitably, yes. I want to experience every bit of happiness with you, no matter the cost I'll bear. I feel as if I've known you for a lifetime, and I don't want this to end. Not now, not ever! You know my feelings, and you know my heart. My heart is yours now, and always will be. I feel as though you feel the same, am I right?"

"Serenity, you're my match in every way. You have my promise to enjoy every bit of this happiness with all my heart. Though, I must tell you one thing before we proceed, in hopes this does not change your mind in any way."

"Nothing can change the way I feel, because I, too, love you."

"First, your sister knows this, and heard the conversation. I asked her not to say anything because I wanted to tell you myself."

"What is it Darien? You're scaring me."

"It's your father."

Her face turned white, and she fought back the tears in her eyes as she listened closely.

Pulling her close, as if to calm her, he replied, "First, listen to all before you comment. Promise me."

She shook her head begrudgingly and said she would.

"I know you are worried about this." She started shaking her head in reply. "I promise you, Serenity, it's going to be okay. Your father has recruited me to fight in this stupid war."

All life fell from her face, and he held her close to calm her worst fear.

In a whisper, all she could muster to say was, "When?"

Chapter 7

Bonding Ties

He wiped the tears from her eyes and said, "I have until the winter's first blanket of snow has fallen." He tilted her eyes to his and said, "We still have the summer, and I'd like to make the most of it. I can't do this alone."

"I hate him! I hate my father for doing this! I hate him…I hate him…I hate him!" She trailed off into a hoarse whisper with tears flowing down her cheeks.

Pulling her close, he said, "I promise you, I will fight my way back to you with every ounce of my life." Lifting her chin to his, his green eyes meeting her clear sky-blue tear-filled eyes, he said, "I needed you to know the truth before anything else. First, can you forgive me for telling you?"

"And second?" she asked.

"Can you put it away in the back of your mind until the time draws near?"

"Darien, on the first, there's nothing to forgive. My father and this *damn* war are to blame for it. On the second, I cannot promise, but I can promise I will try."

"I can live with that." He pulled her back as close as he could, pressing his lips to hers while getting lost in the moment. He pulled back just a little to say in a whisper, intensely holding her gaze, "If this were under normal circumstances, I would have gotten permission from your father to date you. I would have held your hand, taking you for walks along the trails and riding off just to watch the sunsets. Instead, I've found this perfect place, and it's made just for us." Leaning in, he kissed her.

Darien pulled her back as close as he could, pressing his lips to hers while getting lost in the moment, knowing full well this was their first time ever being with anyone. He whispered in her ear passionately. "You are my one true love." Intensely holding her gaze, he softly caressed her lips igniting the fiery kiss.

Serenity, feeling a little nervous yet excited with a burning desire she welcomed the sweet surrender. As he began to remove the straps from her shoulders, caressing lightly with his lips in the bareness of her touch, slowly he moved amorously toward her breast. Her blood pounded in her veins in heated elation losing all her senses spinning with no cares or concerns. He moves inside parting the tightness of her thighs, waters rippling with every thrust. This moment is theirs letting their passion take control emerging their desire as one. Breathing heavily as he kisses her neck slowly moving to her lips under the waterfall's mist. The sparkling crystals illuminating the water caught the dancing rays of sunshine, part of the cave's natural wonder. Their sweltering romance growing more intense, in shallow water, he laid her back just underneath the mist, ravishing the bareness of her breast, sliding into the wetness between her thighs. She softly moaned with every pulse, as he plunged into the maddening clutch in the heat of the moment with her hands locked behind the base of his neck, her breath against his face and the whisper of her voice urging him for more. Whispers in his ear's driving him wild, thrusting harder and faster devouring her soul in heated bliss. Hunger demanding more surging through them to the last arousing euphoria, finishing as he tenderly kisses her lips and pulls her into his arms, carrying her out of the water to a place that is warm after the water's coolness. He laid Serenity in a blanket of pillows, giving her a place of comfort. He caressed her curves and kissed her lips. Her thoughts spun as he held her through the night. He slipped out early, amazed at the love he felt for this beauty, amazed that she had returned *his* love. It was all he had hoped and dreamed of. After a few minutes of gathering something for breakfast, he quietly slipped back next to her after setting down what he gathered. He lightly brushed a strand of hair from her eyes as she stirred and looked upon his face.

"Tell me this is not a dream," she said, looking into his eyes.

Caressing her face, he replied, "No, my love, it is real." He leaned down to kiss her.

With a breath of a whisper she said, "Tell me we can stay here forever."

"Serenity, I wish the same as you. Let's enjoy the time we have, shall we? How about a bite to eat? Thought you might be a little hungry and prepared this for you."

"Perhaps a little bite," she said, knowing she was famished but maintaining her composure.

He set out both red and green seedless grapes, some cheese, smoked sausage, and a few other things, and said, "There's more where this came from."

"When did you gather these? This is really good."

Smiling at her in reply, he said, "I gathered them and pulled them from the cooling room before you woke."

She ate some of the grapes and noticed him watching her eat. She popped one in his mouth and moved to the strawberries. She slowly ate the first, lightly glazing the top of her lips seductively. She took one for him to bite into. As the juice trickled down his chin, she caught the drip from his chin. Then slowly climbed upward to his lips, seductively.

Quickly pulling her close, he kissed her as she forgot about the rest of the fruit.

Stopping before things got out of hand, he said, "Come with me. There's something I want to show you." He pulled her to stand, took her hand, and led her to another area that was just as breathtaking as the first. "How about we go for a swim a little later?"

"Wow! This is so stunning. How many more are there like this? I'd like to see more."

Smiling he said, "Come on, let me show you this area." He led her to a huge cavern, and she was mesmerized by its beauty.

"What is this place? It is so captivating to my eyes."

"If we're really the first to ever see it, how about we call it 'The Jeweled Chasm of Serenity'?" asked Darien.

"How on earth did you come to that conclusion?" she said.

"Here is what I see. Your beauty is beyond measure and those jewels don't hold a candle to it. Your name means peace, and this is a very tranquil place. Besides, your beauty sparkles with such a glow in this chasm, and I shall keep this vision of you wherever I may go."

Reminiscing thoughts filled her mind with what her eyes had already seen of this place, bringing a glow about her face.

Darien said, "This is our place, now and forevermore, of course, as long as you agree."

"Yes, of course I do," she said as she cupped his face softly and tenderly. "Why wouldn't I? Right by your side, I'll be, wherever you may go."

He kissed her lips, while pulling her so close, tightening his grip around her face.

Walking through this chasm, he pulled a flawless blue diamond, perfect in size, to give her. "With this, I'd like to ask your hand in marriage. I fell in love with you the first day I saw your face. My feelings are still the same, and I know they will never change." He got down on one knee, took her hand, and said, "Will you accept my hand in marriage?"

Overwhelmed and in total surprise, she nodded yes, and she threw her arms around him as she whispered, "Yes, I will."

"I have a place for us to go, and I would like you to get only your sister, so we can marry in secret. Can, or more importantly, will you do this?"

"Yes, I can, but my sister is going to flip when she finds out."

"Tell you what. I will take you to your sister behind the grove. Do you remember where that is?"

"Yes," she replied.

"By the way, she told me of an old tradition in your family heritage of long ago. She helped my father and me understand the ways, so that we can do this. My father will be coming to get you when you are ready tomorrow, and I'll take care of the rest, okay?"

"Gosh, it's happening so fast. How are we to keep this from my parents? Wait, my sister knows about this?"

"She only knows what I have planned as a surprise for you. How about we enjoy the rest of today and tonight, so we can just worry about this tomorrow, shall we?" He held out his hand for her to take, and she gladly accepted. Arm in arm, they strolled through this beautifully layered chasm. They walked and talked for hours, looking at all the wonders and baring their souls.

Walking back to the area where they'd first stayed, he said, "I'm going to take you to the springs, where there is a little ventilation for the smoke to escape, undetected. There, we can cook something. Would you like a hot meal?"

"Oh, yes. That sounds delightful. I'm famished."

"You can use these springs if you would like to freshen up a bit, while I get things prepared."

"Don't mind if I do, and I won't take too long. You do think of everything, don't you?" she said coyly, with a smile.

Pulling her close, he said, "For you, I'll do anything," as he kissed her, causing a slight buckle in her knees, weakening her stance as she was intoxicated by his mere presence alone. "I'll be back when I'm finished to get you."

"I'll be in the camp when I am finished here." Smiling, she indulged slipping into the cooling springs beneath the misting waterfall. Gently floating in the shallow water, Serenity relaxed, allowing the water to soothe and refresh her soul. How beautiful the spot. How incredible the feelings that continued to rise in her chest for this noble man, whom she had only recently met, but who had slipped into her life so very quickly that it seemed she had known him…indeed, waited for him, all her life. As the water streamed from her hair, she reached for a soft towel so thoughtfully provided, and then headed to their camp to slip into something more fitting. While waiting, she dozed off to sleep. Darien, coming to take her to where he'd prepared their meal, leaned down and kissed her. Startled, she woke, falling right into the moment. Yes, it was a dream come true.

He picked her up and said, "Come on, let's get you something to eat. I can tell you're hungry."

No arguments as she nodded in reply. As he guided her, she smelled the intoxicating aroma of the roast fowl and sweetened breads he had prepared. As they walked through, she gasped at the beautiful sight.

"Where did you get all of this? You are full of surprises." He just smiled at her and kissed her hand. Candlelight was everywhere reflecting and illuminating the cave.

After they ate, he cradled Serenity in his arms and enclosed them around her.

"Darien, I wish this would never end. I so wish not to return home."

"I feel the same as you. Let's check out those hot springs and not think about it."

"That would be lovely. Don't mind if I do." He took her hand while stepping into the warm water, then pulled her close to him.

Warmly, he embraced her, raising her blue eyes to his and kissing just above her brow. He softly caressed the edge of her face, moving closer, less than inches away. A slight moan escaped from her throat. He pressed his lips to hers in the cascading and iridescent glow from the cave.

Passionately, and weakening her at the knees, he melted her heart with ease. They made love in the forbidden pools. He caressed her every inch, not a moment too soon, never wanting this time to end. The closeness of his breath, the stubble of his chin, the aroma of light sweat caused her blood to pulse. Then he swept her up in a warm embrace, holding her tightly against his strong chest, and carried her through the dimness of their camp.

Lying next to him, she pondered the thought of what would happen if they should ever be caught. A worried expression became prevalent on her face. Lightly, he caressed her, as if to soothe her, and said, "What's wrong? By the look on your face, your thoughts seem miles away."

Shaking her head yes, she uttered one word: "Father."

Softly caressing her lips, as if to shush them, he replied, "Shh shh shh, I assure you, he knows nothing of this place."

Affectionately, he kissed her in an attempt to calm her fears as he held her close by his side.

Looking into her eyes, holding a steady gaze, he took her hand and said, "Marry me in the moonlight when the lights will dance and the moon is full and high. Will you marry me tomorrow night with your sister as a witness? I know not what the war will bring, and I love you more and more. Serenity, I know this is sudden, but fearing I may not have another chance, I needed to ask it again. Knowing your father, he will not permit it. Marrying you may be forbidden under the circumstances, and that is why I wish to do so in secret. I should like to look upon my wife's face to remember while I'm away, not looking back wishing I had done this." He tilted her chin to his as he repeated the words. "No matter how long we've been together, you should know I love you more than life itself. Marry me?"

Throwing her arms around his neck, she replied, "Yes, I'll marry you. Nothing will take away my love for you, not even my father. Although I wish I had the appropriate attire for traditional ceremony."

Putting his lips to hers, he kept her from uttering another word, and then replied, "Don't worry, you will find that your sister knows you well." Smiling while holding her gaze, he said, "Now, where were we?" then gave her no chance to respond.

Breaking for air, in a whisper, she said, "I can't believe my sister knew this and did not even say a word. I'm curious though to know what else she hides from me." With a devious smile, she said, "Is there anything else you wish to confess, or will our lives be filled with secrets?"

"My dear Serenity, know there will be no more secrets, unless you don't mind surprises, or unless"––he paused––"somehow your sister is the only one I can contact, getting through to you, and that would be the only reason. I promise this to you that I will find a way to send you messages while I am away. Can you live with this?"

"My dear soon-to-be husband, I can live with it because the words you speak are in truth. Besides, your eyes don't lie." She gave a hint of a smile as she kissed his lips.

He held her in his arms all night until the morning broke. Waking to the aroma of breakfast, she replied, "That smells divinely heavenly."

While smiling at her, he said, "Thought you might like something good before we meet your sister."

"And just what exactly are our plans today?"

"If you must know, I will tell you this. First, I'll take you to your sister, and she will help you get ready for tonight. In the meantime, I will be preparing for your arrival in a special place. Your sister knows where to take you. Now, you have a lot to do in a very short time."

While smiling at her, he said as he caressed her long soft hair, "Just know I would have done things differently if I could have only had your father's approval. Maybe one day he will open his eyes and see the beauty of the woman before me. Perhaps your mother will finally see the truth behind his secrets." He kissed her in a lasting, passionate moment. "Now, let's eat and go meet your sister."

"I can't believe this is happening. And how my sister pulled this off without even uttering a word is beyond me."

"Serenity, it's really simple. Your sister knows your heart. Even though you had decided that she attend college, she needed you to be happy while she was away. She took a huge risk and chance to see us through. As far as your father goes, I learned of him through my own father, along with the knowledge of what Adriena has provided. We have a lot to do, unless you wish to not go through with this?"

"On the contrary, I do wish to proceed. I love you." She kissed him and held him tightly as she said it.

"Darien, I would like to know how you convinced your father to do this?"

"At first my father didn't approve until I explained what my feelings for you are and what you have told me of you home life. He knew how I felt and knew I would retaliate. My father told me to follow my heart and he would help me any way he could. He knows how happy I am with you and I held nothing back because I needed him to see how I feel. When my mother died a few years back, my father raised me by himself and knew of the loneliness he felt without my mom. We formed a very special bond between father and son. Besides that he knew I would do this anyway, so he gave me his blessing."

He led her to the entrance and asked her to wait while he made sure it was clear to proceed. Then he took her hand, and they went to meet up with Adriena.

Chapter 8

Unbreakable Vow

"Alysa, I must meet my sister and bring her back here. Can you promise me not to say a word to anyone? This is so very important to me and she hasn't a lot of time to do all that's needed before the war. If you knew our father, you would understand why. Now, will you swear to secrecy for my sister's sake?"

"What's going on, Adriena? You're scaring me."

"I'm sorry, Alysa, my father is very overprotective of our family, especially with war upon us. He is not tolerant of some decisions we make, but our mother has given as much help as she can. I'm afraid that, soon, Mother will no longer be able to keep this up, and we are preparing a way to make everything work as best we can. Our family is very different from others."

"What is it I can do to help?"

"You see, I made a vow to my sister and it is an unbreakable bond, this is why I need you to swear secrecy in what I tell you. No one, and I mean no one, can ever know what we are doing. Now, I need you to swear to this, or I will be forced to leave you here and to do what I must. Will you help us?"

"How long must I keep this secret, or what would happen if it came out?"

"Alysa, I know this won't last forever, but if at all possible, at least until after the war. I need friends I can trust. Will you be one of them?"

"Adriena, I swear to whatever you ask of me and that I will not ever say a word to anyone. I, too, value friendship and trust. You are my closest friend. How could I not trust you? Yes, of course I would, without question."

"First, you must know that my father scours these lands. As he searches for new recruits, he searches for places to hide. This is why it has been carefully and strategically put in place by me and Darien. I'll do whatever it takes for my sister, now more than before. I hope you understand why I asked of you in this manner."

"Yes, of course, I understand, Adriena."

"I'm sure by now Darien has asked her and she is headed toward us. We are to meet at the Big Pine of the forest. Then we will bring her back here."

"And then what are we to do?" asked Alysa.

"Preparing her for a secret wedding, of course."

"But she's only known him for a short time, and this is unheard of."

"Alysa, where we come from it is rare, but not unusual in the old days. We are born and raised in the lineage of our ancestors. I'll admit true love is rare, but my sister has it. In the history of our ancestors, it can happen quickly. Later in our history, it became forbidden without approval on both sides, yet it is still prevalent now, only in secrecy. This is called an unbreakable vow. Once they're married, it cannot be undone and will not be taken lightly, which is why I asked for your secrecy. We need to hurry and meet her so they can be ready. I do wish you could attend the ceremony, but in this, it is not allowed. Only his father and I are to attend this, as is tradition."

"Why are you allowed and not one of your parents?"

"Alysa, because our parents forbid it, and I am of age to consent. Be thankful you are not. This can be very dangerous if we are caught. Do you see the magnitude of what I'm asking?"

"Yes, I understand. Serenity is very fortunate to have a sister such as you."

"I would do this without hesitation for anything, for any happiness she can acquire under our father's rule. Now we need to hurry so we can be on time. Are you ready?"

With a smile, Alysa said, "Let's go find your sister."

Through the path, they ran side by side to where they must meet, before stopping dead in their tracks and waiting for the troops passing, and then again hurrying along the way. Quietly, they made their way to the Big Pine, just ahead.

Hugging Serenity, Adriena said, "Sister, it is so good to see you." Looking at Darien, smiling, she said, "And of course, you too."

Darien replied before Serenity answered, saying, "My father will meet you when the time is right. Hurry as fast as you can. We may not have much time in between the patrols."

Not a moment too soon, they hurried to prepare for the unbreakable vow. Serenity's sister did not disappoint as she helped with her attire. A lovely field-flower wreath woven into her beautiful tresses. A lace shawl borrowed from Alysa's mother draped over her shoulders, complementing the ecru color of Serenity's Sunday dress, nearly matching the embroidery and small decorative buttons. Only a hint of sadness crossed her face as she remembered how lovingly this dress had been made for her by their mother. Wishing at this moment that her mother were there sharing in the upcoming ceremony. Finally, without hesitation, Adriena turned to Alysa to say, "Thank you so much for your help. You have no idea how much this means to us."

"Anytime." Alysa turned to Serenity and said, "I wish for you an eternity of happiness in the days to come. I look forward to seeing you again."

Smiling at the words, and tucking the little disappointment deep into her heart, she replied, "Thank you for being ever so kind," and then departed in a hurry to the Big Pine.

Adriena said quietly, "I sure hope his father is there to greet us."

"Me too, Adriena." Stopping them for just a minute, she said, "Thank you for everything you've done." She paused. "I mean it."

"You know I'd do anything for you. We are sisters, are we not?" Before she could reply, they picked up the pace to make it there. As promised, his father was waiting to accompany them the rest of the way.

"You must be Serenity. My son has told me a little about you. He is right about one thing. Your beauty is captivating, and you are most welcomed in our family. My name is Markis Bonnaire, Darien's father, and I am pleased to finally meet you. Thank you for all you have done for my son, Adriena. Let's get you girls to where we are to be. Don't you worry, it will be safe to go where we need to be. My land is well guarded."

Serenity just smiled and looked at Adriena with suspicion at the last remark he made to her.

Adriena whispered to her, "I'll tell you later. I promise."

"Okay, girls, we are here. Adriena, you know what to do."

Right after he left, Serenity was glaring at her sister, and then replied, "Okay, before I go any further, spill it, and don't give me this 'I'll tell you later' bit."

"I told Darien I would need to tell you some of this. You know me too well, and I can't keep it from you any longer. The last time at the lake, I told you I was going to see our friend. Not all of that was accurate. I did go see Alysa, though I did not stay long. I went to Darien's father, as he asked me to. From there, we set this up as much

57

as we could. It was supposed to be a surprise. Knowing you, I didn't think we could make it all the way through without telling you. Now you know. I wish you both so much happiness, and I'm jealous you get to experience it all first." Hugging her sister, she said, "Now, we need to get over there, or he will send a search party to get us." Both of them started laughing.

"All right, Adriena, I forgive you for this, and I'm glad you're here to share this with us. The beauty of this place is just breathtaking," gasped Serenity as they ran beneath the cedar trees.

Adriena took her right to Markis as he walked down the path to greet her. The strong father figure held out his arm for her to take as they made their way down a pine-needle path with small tapers of light to each side until there stood, only a few feet away from the ceremony's focus, a small arbor graced with white day lilies, which seemed to have just bloomed ever so perfectly for this occasion. Continuing on, Markis escorted her to Darien for that one final walk down the now petal-strewn aisle.

Elaborate secret weddings were very rare to see and very short in the ceremony.

After the unbreakable vows were said, with seeming shortness of breath, which Darien had not yet experienced, he leaned closely to Serenity and boldly said:

Serenity, I take you to be my wife.

A radiant sight that I behold
My love, my life forever more
I, Darien, decree my love to Serenity
An unchained melody that I adore

My promise to respect and trust
With my undying love forever

I give you my heart and soul
Our unbreakable vow together

Though these times will not be easy
My desire, my love within my heart
Binding ties will never waver
As long as we live, let no one depart

You're the peace within my storm
For everything that we shall face
I love you, Serenity, with all my heart
It is here and now, my eternal embrace

Serenity whispered her response as tears pressed close…
Darien, I take you to be my husband.

Beguiling my senses right from the start
My love, my life forevermore
I, Serenity, decree my love to Darien
Whose depth and character I adore

My promise to respect and trust
With my undying love forever
I give you my heart and soul
Our unbreakable vow together

Though these times will not be easy
My desire, my love within my heart
Binding ties will never waver
As long as we live, let no one depart

You're the peace within my storm

For everything that we shall face
I love you, Darien, with all my heart
It is here and now, my eternal embrace

They lit a unity candle from two separate candles prepared for exactly that purpose, signifying that the light of their lives, yes, even their souls, were now forever one.

Darien turned to Serenity and kissed his new bride. As tears streamed down Adriena's face, she was very happy for her sister and new brother-in-law.

Now, formally secretly wed by the old ways, they said a few words before they left. Serenity hugged her sister one last time as they said their goodbyes. Markis turned to Serenity and said, "You are most welcome to our family, and I am proud and happy to have you as my daughter. You will, without a doubt, be good to my son. Don't hesitate to come to me for any reason, if you need me." After he hugged her, he turned to Adriena and escorted her back to camp while Darien took Serenity back to their hidden paradise.

Chapter 9

Secret Binding

Markis turned to Adriena to say, "I want to thank you for everything you've done to help me make this happen. It is a joy to see such happiness on my son's face once again. I had despaired of seeing him smile with such contentment since the passing of his mother a few years back. Though this will not be easy for either of them at this young age and as war rages toward us. I pray we survive this, so you and they can experience the joy and peace for a lifetime to come. I am at peace, my son has his life now. You are an extraordinarily fine young woman. May your life be filled with the happiness you deserve."

"I'm flattered by your kind words, Mr. Bonnaire. I believe you meant every word. I would do anything for my sister, and it brings me joy to see that her happiness is fulfilled. It is a pleasure to know your son, who is very much like his father, the perfect gentleman. Serenity could not have ever found a better man and family in her life. Thank you for helping me with this."

"Jusqu'à ce que nous nous revoyions."

"I'm afraid I haven't learned the language. Can you indulge me with what it says?"

"It means till we meet again. Goodbye for now."

Adriena was surprised at the fatherly hug and kiss on each cheek.

When she finally returned, Alysa asked, "Did everything come together well? I bet it was beautiful."

"Oh, Alysa, it was so magical. My sister is so happy, and I am dreading the trip back home. This will not be easy for either of us."

"Do you know where they are?"

"No, I haven't a clue. Wherever they are, knowing Darien, it will be blissful heaven on earth. The less we know where, the better off they are."

"Any ideas on where your father is lately?"

"Mr. Bonnaire said his men are patrolling the perimeter. He spotted him about five days away on the other side of his land. He hasn't been on the move as of yet, but will let me know as soon as he knows. As of right now, we are safe."

"Do you think your mother suspects anything?"

"She knows my sister is in love, as of right now. When we arrive home, I'm afraid that will change. Our mother has a way of finding things out. I'm sure she will notice great changes in my sister. I just hope we can convince her otherwise."

"What do you think will happen if you do not?"

"It will be very difficult for my sister to return and see Darien. I'm constantly trying to come up with new things and ways. Oh, why can't we just have a normal life? I hate this. I wish this damn stupid war would never start, but my ever-so-lovely father just has to make sure it does, just to add to his valor of loyalty. I so hope Darien can withstand what is coming."

"What do you really think is coming?'

"I really wish not to think of this. Can we discuss something else?"

"Yes, of course, my apologies. I didn't mean to press. I went home to get a few more provisions for our stay here, and my father asked if we were coming to the dance at the end of the week."

"What was your reply?"

"I kind of told him we would be there. Hope you don't mind."

"That should work out perfectly. My sister should be returning by then, provided there are no more surprises."

"Good, then this should all work out."

"I sure hope so, Alysa. I really do. Want to see if we can catch some fish?"

"Sure, and the coolness of the water would feel good and refreshing." They grabbed their things while laughing, and, after sharing a best-friend hug, they made their way.

Chapter 10

New Ties

Finally reaching the entrance, Darien swept Serenity up in his arms to carry her through. Startled at the swiftness of his movement, she gasped and giggled. He said, while gazing into her eyes, "This may not be home, but it is our place, and will remain for as long as we can hide it." Once they were through the entrance, he kissed her lips as her feet touched the floor. Holding her in a warm embrace, he guided her to another place. While covering her eyes, he said, "No peeking. Don't open until I say."

"I won't. Besides, I can't see a thing."

"Good, let's keep it that way."

"Where on earth are you taking me?"

With her heart aflutter at the excitement, he said, "Just a little further. We're almost there. Now, feel my movement and watch your step as we step down just a bit." As he helped her along the way, he said, "That's it. You're doing great." He picked her up, and wrapped his arms tightly around her as she clung around his neck, feeling the bulging of his muscles. Setting her carefully down on soft pillows and blankets beneath them, he said "Open your eyes."

Encased by the beauty within their surroundings, she let out a gasp of surprise in her voice. "Oh, Darien, just when I thought it couldn't get better than what we've seen." The cave had been carpeted. There were sconces set in the walls to light the interior. Flowers were strewn on the floor that created a wonderful perfume as the petals were pressed underfoot. This was by far the most enchanting. He turned his eyes to look at her. Kissing him with deep affection, she whispered, "Oh, how much I do love you."

He pressed down harder on her lips as he quickly removed the dress she had on, livening up with the abundance of her breasts and ravishing her bareness sliding his hands between her legs. The rhythm of their hearts elevated with excitement escalating into a breathless rapture. With the warmth of his skin caressing her own, into a delicious torment tantalizing the caress of her exquisite tightness between her thighs, she yearns the need escalating into a heated passion. He penetrated deeper as he gazed into her smoldering blue eyes and deepened his kiss. With every swiftly paced thrust, she gasped for air, and her body exploded into an elation she had never before known. She moaned in an echo with each penetrating thrust and ecstasy up until the last release. He kissed her lips in heated desire, making her want more. He held her tight in a warm embrace. Resting for a bit with his gaze upon her beauty's blush, his light touch moved a strand of hair from her eyes. "Your eyes are the radiance of the rising sun, a beauty which I love to look upon," he said poetically with his lips lightly grazing her brow.

She met his gaze as she says, "Your words are tantalizing, lighting fire deep within my soul. I never knew how much joy this could bring, gazing upon the one I love so much."

Softly caressing her lips between words, he repeated, "Mon amour… Mrs. Bonnaire"

In a soft whisper she said, "I like the sound of that."

He replied, "My heart is everlasting, my love is eternal, to know I will remember the look upon your face no matter where it is I go.

Let's enjoy what time we have and know that I will find my way back to you. Someway, somehow."

She reached for the biggest strawberry and teased him as she bit it while juice ran down the center of her chin. Shaking his head, penetrating her fiery gaze, he said in a whisper, "No, that will not do." With the tip of his tongue, he started at the bottom of the drip and moved up, until he met her lips with a blaze, bringing a shiver to the light of his touch, heightening her arousal in ecstasy through the night.

Alysa asked Adriena the next morning, "What would you like to do today? Want to help me get the area set up for the dance we're having in a few weeks? Looks like we have a lot of work to do."

"Sounds like a good idea. Don't have to worry about my sister, she's in good hands. She is blessed to have this going for her, and he is really good to her," she said, smiling at the thought.

"You wish it was happening to you, don't you? I can't believe your sister would go so fast. That just doesn't happen here."

"Yes, I do wish I had what my sister has, yet I am so happy for her, and wouldn't change a thing. It is not uncommon for our family line to find true love, but it is rare in the way this has been. When war's upon us, it makes a huge difference to factor in. We really had hoped to have had more time. Unfortunately, that was not in the equation. It is a long road to come. I know she will never regret this decision. Besides, once set in motion, it cannot be undone. It is for life, no matter what the circumstance may be. Not even our father can change it, but if he finds out too soon, it will make our lives even more difficult. I intend to do everything I can to keep that from happening. Will you help me where you can?"

"Yes, of course I will, Adriena. I'm here for you any time you need me or ask for it."

"I know this is asking a lot, and I wouldn't ask it if this were not as important as it is."

"Adriena, it's okay. Really, I mean it."

"Alysa, who is coming to this dance? Anyone we know?"

"Do you remember Jothan and Vaughan?"

"I sure do. Vaughan was really sweet, not to mention cute!"

"They will be coming. I think Vaughan fancies you. Will your sister and Darien be here?"

"Better be. Our mother is coming. I am worried about Mother's reaction."

"You really think your mother will have that kind of reaction?"

"I know if my sister can't hide the way she feels well enough, Mother will not be tolerant. Heaven forbid our father finds out any of this. I just hope we see Serenity before anyone else does."

"Agreed, now let's not worry about this and see what we can get accomplished. I'd like to see if we can catch any fish to have with the rest of the trimmings for dinner. If, of course, you agree."

"Fine by me. Let's get this finished." Working for two hours, they set the stage with some new decorations. After finishing, they left to go fishing.

"Adriena, maybe we can catch something today. Then cook them over the fire pit. Sounds lovely."

"Yes, it does. What kind of dance will this be? We don't get to dance much, though we enjoy it when we do."

"It's a mixture of folk and tribal dance off and on throughout the summer. Have you not heard of it before?"

"Honestly, Alysa, that is what our father taught us growing up. It's a rendition of the folk dance of the Neachean people. It's my understanding you have to be of noble blood or of the Neachean people to participate?"

"Technically, we are not, but my father was taught in secret long ago by one of noble blood. He decided to hold this dance on our land so he would never forget it. He taught me from the time when I was very young. How do you know of it?"

"We are of noble blood. My father served the royal guard. When he married our mother, he was exiled because she was not. Now, he is head of the Neachean Force, a brutal force, and no one dares to question his authority."

"Wait a minute! You were born of noble birth? The noble bloodline's coursing through your veins?"

"Actually, we are half. Our mother is not of noble birth, though by rights through marriage she should be. Our father treats her as though she is the same."

"Adriena, this dance is going to be epic. To me, the dance is intriguing. Even more so when someone understands the same as I."

"Alysa, you do know Darien is of noble birth in his family line. My father will be furious when he finds out they were married in secret and now bonded. My sister knows well the risks and is prepared to face them, should the need arise. Such an alliance is forbidden, but he is married to our mother, which is enough to allow this to be. We had it done in secret was so he could not contest it. We are hoping one day he will accept it."

"Wow, I had no idea. I shall not utter a word at all, Adriena. You have my word. For her sake, I hope he does accept it."

"You understand why we had to conceal this from you until it was safe to tell you? It will not be easy for us, especially for my sister. We have planned out what we need to, should the need arise. My only concern is that my sister does not reveal this too soon."

"Forgive me for asking. What would happen if it were too soon?"

"Alysa, I really don't know. All I do know is my father is very unpredictable. I intend for him not to find out, if at all possible."

"Understood. Do you know how your mother and father met?"

"Remind me again when the worst has passed, and I will tell you then. Okay?"

"My apologies. I didn't mean to pry."

"On the contrary, Alysa, I would tell you now if it were better times. As it is, I must be wary of what I say and do. Hope you understand the reason."

"I do. Now how about we take what we have and go cook them. I'm starved."

Both laughed as they gathered the fish and made their way back to camp.

Chapter 11

Bittersweet

Holding Serenity close, wiping tears from her eyes, Darien says, "I know. I wish the same as you. Remember, you are strong, and you have your sister to help you through while we are apart. I will see you as much as I can. Trust your sister. She will see to it that we do." He lifted her eyes to him, and affectionately kissed her. Departing slowly, he took her hand and said, "Shall we? We do still have a dance to make, and I intend to dance with you," and smiled at her.

With a slight smile, she said, "If we must."

"After the dance, I will find a way to you again, and I hope it will be very soon. My father will do what he can to help with your father so that we can spend as much time together as possible."

Stopping him just for a minute or so, she said, "Darien, I'm not good at hiding things from my mother. She can read me like an open book. What am I to do?"

"Serenity, worst case would be if she were to tell your father. As long as we can keep this from happening, we should be fine. From what your sister has told me your mother looks after the both of you more than you know. Let's just see how long we can do this. We will have to face it eventually, so let's enjoy what time we do have."

"Perhaps you're right. You know I can't help but worry. Though I'll continue to do so, I will do my best to accommodate."

70

"That's my girl, I know you can do this. Let's be on our way or your sister will be frantic."

Smiling at the thought, she said, "I suppose you're right. We should hurry."

To speed their time, Darien's father had left some horses for faster travel. Cautiously, they wound through the trees so as not to make a sound, then carefully slowed to stop as they approached to walk the rest of the way. Just out of sight, shielded by a screen of wild lilac bushes, he pulled her close. Affectionately, he kissed her, weakening her stance.

Breaking the hold just for a moment, breathlessly she said, "You keep that up and you won't leave so easily."

Smiling as his eyes lit up, he responded by lightly caressing her neck, and then with a teasing kiss. "You read me well. Not easy at all. Come on, let's grace the girls with our presence."

Adriena, standing in the shadows, stepped out and said, smiling, "You should get a room. Oh, look, we have two."

Serenity hugged her sister, saying, "I know it's been only a week. I have missed you too."

Returning the hug to her sister, Adriena replied, "Good to see you took good care of my sister. Won't you stay for a while? At least have a bite to eat? We have plenty."

"Okay, you've convinced me. Just for a little while," he said, looking at Serenity with a smile.

Adriena picked up on Darien's response and said, "It's okay. You don't have to pretend around us. Alysa knows."

With comfort in mind, he pulled Serenity close, locking his arms around her.

Startled by his movement, Serenity smiled with a devious grin.

Adriena laughed at their display and said, "Come on, I'm starved."

Alysa, looking up, noticed, and replied, "I just took up the last of it. Why don't we go inside to the table?"

They talked for a while after they ate, and then Darien bid his farewell. Pulling Serenity close, he kissed her feverishly, and then said, "Until I see you again," and goodbye in his language, "Jusqu'à ce que je vous revoyions. Au revoir."

Sadly, not wanting him to leave her side, she responded with a tearful goodbye, whispering how much she loved him.

She knew that Adriena was waiting to bombard her with a million questions, which she knew to carefully answer. She stood and watched him until she could no longer see him through the shadows. Serenity slowly turned her face with streaked cheeks and wiped her eyes. Facing her sister, she said, "I so hate keeping this silent."

"I know, Serenity, we will find a way to get you back to him again, soon. At least you can see him tomorrow night. Just be careful when you dance to the tribal tune. Mom can see right through us."

"Adriena, how well do I know, and it will not get any easier. Just hope we can elude them long enough."

"True enough, and I can see how much you do love him. So tell me, where did you go?"

"I'm sorry, Adriena, I can't reveal where we went because it is hidden well. I can tell you it was so magical. The place would just blow your mind. I didn't want to leave at all. The water was perfect and would take your breath away." Her face was glowing as she told it.

Just as Adriena began to respond, Alysa stepped out for their attention. "Hey, are you going to stay outside all night or come inside?"

Smiling at Adriena, Serenity said in a whisper, "I'll just have to tell you later."

Adriena replied, "Our apologies, Alysa, we are coming in just a moment."

Taking Serenity by the arm, she smiled and said, "Come, let's get ourselves inside before we get drilled with more questions to answer. She knows some of what is going on. Remember, some, not all, so choose your words wisely in your response."

"Understood, Adriena. I can do this, and I hope it is easier somehow."

"Don't worry, I'll help you as much as I can. Besides, we're in this together," Adriena said seriously, with a smile.

They went in and stayed up for a while, talking about the dance taking place the following night.

Darien returned home to let his father know he was there. "Father, I'm home. Oh, my apologies," he said, as he bowed to his father's company. "I wasn't aware we had company."

"Son, you remember Commander Kozlov?"

"I believe so, though we've not formally met. I only know of what my father has told me, which is very little." Shaking his hand, he said, "Nice to finally meet you."

"Darien, he is here on official business."

"Thank you, Markis, I'd like to talk with Darien alone."

"Yes, of course. I'll be in the guest house when you are finished."

"Very well." Waiting till Darien's father could no longer hear, the commander began, "Darien, first of all, I had hoped this could wait another month or so. However, I need you to report to active duty under my command one month from now. When I leave, just be ready to join us as we make our way back here. Is that understood?" he said robustly and sternly.

Saluting under his command, Darien said, "Yes, sir."

"You have one month to get your things in order until we leave. Your father knows of this importance and will treat it as such."

"Understood, sir," Darien replied with a salute.

"I'm sorry, Son, but we need every available able-bodied man." Pulling himself up on the horse, he said, "I'll return one month from now. Be ready."

"Yes, sir."

Darien's father returned to comfort his son. "I'm sorry, Son. I had hoped there would be more time. Believe me, I'd do anything to prolong it. As it is out of my hands, with that said, spend as much time with her as you can. She will need comfort while you're away. I pray for your safe return, so you can have the family you deserve. I love you, Son, and you mean the world to me."

Darien replied, "I hate this. She doesn't deserve any of this." Choking on unshed tears, he said, "I need to be alone to collect my thoughts." He instantly stormed out the door and galloped off on his favorite horse.

"D-a-r-i-e-n." The sound echoed in his ears, his father's anguished call.

Darien did not reply, and kept on going until he was out of sight. Not heeding the heartbreak of his father, as his own breaking heart washed waves of pain over him, he was grateful for the comfort of his trusted steed, always warm and true.

Chapter 12

Beyond Bounds

Carefully, Darien slowed his stride as he approached almost too closely to Serenity's father. He watched to make sure it was clear and to know where the commander advanced before he proceeded going forward. Her father appeared to be in deep thought and seemed to be headed back home.

He made his way to Serenity as soon the way was clear, risking all to talk to her and Adriena.

With the lights still on, he knocked on the door. Adriena peeked to see who it was. She scrambled to open the door as she said, "It's Darien! What in the world are you doing back so soon, and at this time of night!"

"Please, may I come in?"

"Why yes, yes of course."

He hugged Serenity tightly as he said, "I'm sorry. I just had to see you before night settles in."

Obviously knowing something was wrong, with a quiver in her voice, she replied, "What is it? What's wrong, Darien? You're scaring me."

"Remember, I promised you no more secrets, and your sister must hear this, as this will affect her as well."

"Darien? What's going on?

"Sh, sh, sh," he said, hugging her tightly against his thundering heart, then holding her face in his hands, looking intently into her eyes. "Listen to me, for this is not easy for me to say. I was intending to talk to my father as soon as I arrived."

Adriena's color left her face, as she knew this was not good.

"When I walked in, your father was there."

With flowing tears, Serenity ran outside, not wanting to hear the rest, saying, "No, not now!"

Darien ran after her, with Adriena right on his heels.

Between sobs, she said, "Why! Why now! Why does he have to ruin everything! Why can't things be normal! Damn this *war*!" She hit his chest with her fist in anger. He pulled her tight, bringing her close to him, not letting go until she calmed down.

Slowly, she looked at him with tear-filled eyes and said, in a hoarse whisper, "When? Just tell me when? How much time do we have?"

He paused for a moment and then said, "Calm down, Serenity. Please, calm down."

In tears of anger, she yelled, "When! Tell me when, damn it!"

Not holding back, he said, "One month from today. We have only one month, and I'm to report to do my duty under his command."

He held her tightly as she yelled, "Let me go!" until her voice was a whisper and she'd quelled her anger. He caressed her hair back from her tear-stained face, while Adriena and Alysa were held speechless at what they'd just heard.

After Serenity calmed down, she looked at him with sadness and said, "Please don't leave. Stay here. Stay with me."

"I'll stay until you fall asleep. I must go back to my father as quickly as I can. I'm sure he is worried, and I did not say where I was going. Please don't worry. I will be back as soon as I can, early tomorrow." He kissed her, then laid his forehead against hers and said, "I promise you, I will return. We still have a month, and I intend to use it wisely."

After going back inside and discussing what they would do, he began to walk out the door. Standing at the door, as if to knock, was Darien's father with something in his hands.

"Father! What are you doing here? What is this you have?"

"I had a feeling you would come here. I brought you some attire to change into for tomorrow."

"Why? I was about to come home and explain my actions."

"No need for that, Son. I understand. Stay here." Looking at Serenity, he said, "She needs you. Her mother won't be here until late, so you have plenty of time." As he looked at her sister and Alysa, he said with a stern voice, "I trust nothing will be said to anyone about what is and has been discussed. Right, girls?"

Both replied, "Yes, sir. Not one word at all."

"Good, let's keep it that way. I'd best be on my way. I need to be up early to feed our keep." Looking at Serenity and Adriena, he said, "I am truly sorry. I will do everything I can to make sure you have as much time as you can. I promise you, I will try." He bowed to them as he took his leave.

Adriena and Alysa stayed in one room, being that there were only two available, while Darien and Serenity took the other.

Adriena said to Alysa, "I'll take the floor. We have plenty of blankets for comfort."

"Are you sure? I don't mind taking the floor at all."

"No, it's okay. Besides, it won't matter where we sleep."

"Why do you say this?"

"Honestly, I don't think we will be getting much sleep," Adriena said, raising her eyebrows and pointing next door.

Laughing, she replied, "Oh! I guess not, but we can try."

Darien took Serenity into the other room. While looking at her, he used his thumbs to wipe away her tears. "I promise you, I will find my way back to you. Let's enjoy what we have, right here and now." Kissing her to calm her thoughts, he said in a whisper, "Your father can't take away what we have, Mrs. Bonnaire, now can he? I'm going to enjoy my beautiful wife."

With a radiance flowing through her face, dancing blue eyes glowing in the moonlight through the window, he pulled her in a tight embrace. Before she could say another word, feverishly he pressed his lips to hers, sweeping Serenity from her feet. Darien lays her on the mattress beneath them and removing every piece of clothing without a word between them. Quickly, he slid his hand between her thighs working his fingers through her crease. She forgot about anyone that could hear them as she lost herself into her own pleasure releasing a moan of sweet elation from her voice panting louder, contracting her thighs against his hand. The muscles in her legs began to tense, quivering as he felt her contract against his body. He slipped inside her before she could recover ravishing the tightening heat in exquisite bliss embracing her fully engaged in the moment.

They let all of their passion ignite, hunger surging through her wanting more.

Breaking away just for a moment, in a whisper she said, "What about them? They will hear."

Hushing her with a kiss, he replied, "I'm here for you, not them. I think they will understand." He smothered her with kisses, covering every inch, loving with everything he had to give.

With a radiance flowing through her face, dancing blue eyes glowing in the moonlight, they let all of their passion ignite until the final thrust.

He kissed her brow and pulled her close, and held her through the night, till the morning's light.

Serenity awakened to his eyes fixed upon her, smiling as he kissed her good morning.

He said, "I'm going to take a dip in the lake to freshen up a bit. Would you care to join me?"

"Now? Won't it be a little brisk?"

"Perhaps, though with you there, I'm sure it will warm up a bit, don't you think?"

Kissing him at the thought, she said, "I'm blown away by your romancing notions. You spoil me."

"I'll spoil you every chance I get, just to see that smile upon your face, lighting those dancing blues."

Serenity walked out of the room with her face flushed with radiance and her sister did not miss what she saw. Adriena smiled at how happy she was, and replied, "Just where do you think you're going?"

Darien, cleared his throat and responded, "We're going to the lake to refresh for the day."

"Now? At this time of the morning? Don't you think it a bit chilly?"

"Yes, of course. It will warm not long after, though." He looked at Serenity, smiling.

Adriena and Alysa did not miss a thing, and the blush on Serenity's face began to deepen in awkwardness.

Darien broke the sudden silence, saying, "We won't be long. Besides, we'll be back before lunch and before anyone begins to show."

"Shouldn't you at least eat a bite before you go?" Adriena said.

"I have just what we need along the way. You worry too much. We will be fine." Darien gave her a wink as he said it.

"Just looking out for my sister. I can see there's no worries," Adriena said with a smile. "Make sure you're back before Mom shows."

Looking at Adriena, Darien said, "My father has that covered, so we will be okay."

Serenity spoke up, looking at him, and said, "You do think of everything, don't you?"

"For you? Anything, my love."

Adriena replied, "All right, go on. Before you need another room."

On that note, breaking with laughter, they departed.

Romancing in the waters of Bojovník Lake, tail of the Warrior Lake, Darien and Serenity were refreshed by its chill. Reluctantly, they headed back to eat dinner and ready themselves for the big dance, where close families came to mingle.

"It's about time you showed. We were going to send a search party!" Adriena said.

Darien winked at her as he replied, "You know she's in good hands. Besides, we're here, are we not?"

Giving him a devious look, she said, "I suppose, but you could have been here earlier, and we could have used some help with lunch."

Darien had one of his father's men help bring in some provisions as he said, "Will this help?"

Adriena said, "Where in the world did you get all of this?"

"My father sent it," said Darien.

"Wow! With this much food, we won't have any room for tonight. Never mind on the help. You sure know how to make an entrance."

He was surprised as Adriena said it. "My father will be bringing the provisions for tonight, so we won't have to do anything."

"Why would he do this?" Adriena replied.

"In celebration of our union. Only we will be aware of it, and it must remain this way, so not a word."

"Yes, of course. It's very kind of your father to go out of his way to do this, and I'm sure it is much appreciated," Adriena replied at his generosity.

Alysa walked in to say, "Everything is set and I'm famished. What is all of this?"

"Darien's father sent it. Come on. Let's put this somewhere. I'm sure we have room for it," Adriena replied.

In shock at the abundance, Alysa helped.

Serenity looked at Darien and said, "I love your father. Just as his son." She kissed him while saying, "Perfect gentlemen, you are."

Adriena walked in before it really heated up and said, "All right, come on, let's eat. You really need to separate or this will never work."

He smiled as he took Serenity by the hand to follow. They ate and readied for the dance.

Chapter 13

Tie Dance

Adriena told Serenity how they must enter to be less conspicuous. "Serenity, you are to walk in with Alysa and me, while Darien walks in with his father. We will have to do our best with what is at hand and as we go. I believe we'll be fine, though the dance may prove otherwise. You will need to fight hard to control your emotions."

Darien looked at them with a grim face and said, "My father told me your father will be here for a short time. It is my understanding he is not going to stay through the entire dance. My concern is to make it through the time he is here. Do you think this will be possible?"

Serenity replied, "As long as he leaves before the Tie Dance. I don't feel I can make it."

"Why not?" Alysa asked.

"Darien, Adriena knows I lose myself in this, and I have no control. Be warned of my actions ahead of time."

"She's right, Darien," Alysa said. "She will need you to help her stay focused."

Serenity said, "Alysa, I'm afraid that won't do. Darien will enhance that dance, making it harder to focus on anything at all."

"We will just have to make it through until your father leaves. There is just no other way," Darien replied and then said, "There is one more thing. The reason your father is coming is to announce mine and a few others' departure that will be taking place. My belief is after the announcement he is to take his leave from the dance."

Alysa spoke her thoughts. "Guys, why don't we just have fun without the seriousness, as if nothing has transpired. We can do this."

Darien walked in with his father, going past Serenity's parents with a salute and a bow and a very brief "Hello."

Commander Kozlov replied, "I trust you will be ready when the time comes."

Markis replied, "Can we please leave business where it belongs? Let them enjoy tonight, and make your speech very brief so they can do so."

"But of course, Markis. I meant no disrespect. I will do as you wish for now."

"Thank you, sir. That is all I ask," he replied with sternness in his voice. "When are we to hear your speech?"

"After the first dance. I intend to have one dance with my wife before I leave."

"Very well," Markis replied.

Noticing the friction between their fathers, Darien dared not to say a word. Then he walked toward the girls, and spoke very briefly. "Adriena, I think this will work." Then he looked at Serenity and said, "Forgive me. In order for this to work, I'll need to dance with your sister first. Do you have any objections? I promise, it is just one dance."

"No objections, yes, of course, do what you must."

"And you, Adriena?"

"No objections." And she looked at her sister to say, "It is a good idea. Well planned, and I believe this will work."

Darien said, "Very well. Your father plans to have one dance, make his announcement, and as I understand, be on his way for more important business he is to attend."

With every ache in his bones, Darien stood away from Serenity and dared not to get any closer. He went back to his father and waited for the music to start.

"Careful, Son. Just a little longer. I know you can do it," Markis replied to Darien. All the while Serenity's father's eyes were intently fixed on them.

"Why does he have to stare at us like that? Makes me uneasy just being here."

"Dominance, Son. Don't let it frighten you. He is, after all, your father-in-law."

"I know, Father. Still doesn't make it any easier."

"Just remember the one you truly love. She will sustain you," Markis replied to his son.

"Yes, Father."

Alysa's father made his way for their attention as he announced, "Gentlemen, take your stance in front of whom you'll dance with."

"Go, Son, make me proud." With half a grin, he walked swiftly before the music began. He took his bow to Adriena as she curtsied before him while her father took her mother to the floor to do the same.

Looking dead at Adriena, he said, "I should like to speak with you after my speech is made."

Nervously, she replied, "Yes, Father."

Her father made his way to the other side, his eyes not wavering from her.

Darien whispered, "Stay calm and let him say what he will."

Adriena looked at him and said, "Tell that to my nerves."

He said to her, "If anyone can do it, you can. I have faith in you. Stay calm for your sister."

Just as the music began, she replied, "I wish I could say the same."

Markis danced with Serenity as he tried to keep her calm. The music changed and they switched about.

As Darien briefly danced with his new wife, he said to her, "Steady and calm, you can do it." Which brought a smile briefly, until she saw her father's gaze, and it immediately faded away.

Music faded as they returned to their spots while their father took center stage.

Serenity looked at her sister to say, "What did Father say?"

"It's nothing, he just wanted to speak with me after his speech. Don't worry, I can handle it."

As their father looked at all the young men that had come, he announced their departure in one month from today. He told them to be ready for when it was time. Never breaking his gaze, he said to them, "Adriena, Serenity, I'd like to talk with you alone."

Both said, "Yes, Father."

"Now, Adriena, I hear you orchestrated this camping excursion knowing the severity of this war. Because of the location, I will allow it until I make my leave in a month. Is that understood?"

"Yes, Father," both replied.

"Oh, one more thing. You are to stay away from Darien. Is that understood? I know of your visits to the lake, and don't think it will go unnoticed. Is that understood?"

Swallowing hard, fighting back tears, Serenity nodded unwillingly, as did Adriena.

"How long do you girls plan to camp?"

Adriena spoke up to say, "If we are to have only a month left, then we should like to make the most of it. Then we will do as you say."

"Very well. I'll allow it only because your mother says it does you good. I only want what's best for my daughters, and I do love you. Be warned, do not cross me and take advantage of the **leniency I've given you.** Understood?"

Both girls answered together, "Yes, Father."

Serenity replied, "Will that be all, Father?"

"Yes, you may return to the dance."

As soon as he was out of view, Serenity looked at Adriena and said, "Please excuse me. I need to use the ladies' room." She fought the tears as she moved swiftly to find it.

Adriena immediately told Darien what had transpired. He ran swiftly and discreetly to her side, along with Adriena.

"Serenity, let me in," Darien said, knocking on the door.

She opened the door slowly to let them in. Holding her tightly, he said, "Don't worry, we will find a way. I have some ideas to tell you, but not here." He lifted her chin to kiss her.

Adriena cleared her throat and said, "I'll wait out here and keep an eye on things."

He only half heard what she said and deepened their kiss. Then Darien stopped to say, "We still have a dance and I'd like to have at least one with you."

She had a smile on her face. He always knew how to take away her sadness.

"Do you feel ready to head back?" asked Darien.

"Yes, I believe so. I'm okay," said Serenity.

"He didn't say we had to start tonight, now did he? Let's enjoy what we can, right here and now, shall we?"

Alysa came running in and saw the grim look on their faces. She didn't question, instead saying, "Only one song left to play. If you are going to dance, you need to join in on the last one coming up. They are getting ready to play it."

Darien replied, "We are coming, Alysa." Then he turned to Serenity, saying, "Are you ready?"

"Yes, of course, I wouldn't want to miss it. Besides, it might be the only dance we have." He kissed her hand as they walked out the door and never let it go.

Reminiscing lovers of a hidden past as they are held within a dance forbidden by many in a song is compelling to hear and see.

Though Serenity's father left, her mother remained in the shadows to see if her intuition was true. She knew Adriena was putting on a front with her father. Until now, she hadn't known why. She watched as Serenity and Darien danced, closely knit with the tone of the language brought forth. Seeing this brought memories of things she'd thought never would be seen again. Secrets of the past revealed in a dance only so few could see. She left for home, having seen all she needed with all thoughts of her own she had.

Radiance flowed through Darien and Serenity, locking eyes in an intense moment like there was no one else in the room. Adriena worried about them drawing too much attention. It was the last dance and she was just glad their father wasn't here to see it. Flawlessly dancing to the lover's tune. Adriena breathed a sigh of relief that it was over.

One final turn ended the dance, leaving them desiring each other even more.

Chapter 14

Disarrayed

Just making it back, Darien swiftly lifted Serenity from her feet and took her back to the room. He kissed her, leaving barely enough room for air. Serenity replied in a breathless whisper, "What about them?"

Swiftly removing each garment, he said, "They will understand and after that dance, I intend to ravish my wife." He kissed her in between words. "Inch…by…inch." Nothing else was ever said.

Slowly walking back to the cabin, Adriena spoke. "Alysa? What did your father say to you just before we left?"

Hesitating at first, she said, "He said that I should stay away from those that harbor secrets in love."

"He knows what transpired through that song and dance?"

"Yes, Adriena, it seems that he does. Not to worry, only very few will know."

"My worry is not of the few that know, but of the few that are loyal to my father."

"Do you really think someone there would say something?"

"I don't really know, Alysa. I need to speak with Darien's father. He may be able to help, and is the only one I would trust to do so."

"Right now?"

"Yes, the quicker the better. Hurry! Let's get our horse and see if we can catch him. He shouldn't be that far ahead."

They rode quickly through the night, grateful that there was a bright moon and the galaxy of stars above. A soft breeze was at their back, helping to propel them along, as if all the forces of nature were conspiring with them to provide the quickest overtaking of Markis. They saw him through the trees and slowed their horses to a trot and pulled up right up next to him.

"Adriena, what in heaven's name brings you this far and at this time of night?"

"Sir," Adriena said. "I mean no disrespect. I've come to ask a favor. Please, sir, will you listen?"

"Of course. If it is something I can be of assistance with, I will certainly try. Now, what is it, my dear?"

Alysa told of what her father said and Adriena filled in the rest.

"Adriena, I assure you, I will do everything in my power that no harm will come to any of you. Technically, that cabin is on our land, and I'll have my men be on the lookout for anything suspicious, okay? Try not to worry. One more thing. If you will be so kind as to tell my son I wish to see him, you, and Serenity, to discuss some things that are needed, I'd be much obliged."

"Yes, sir, and what time would you like to see us?"

"Late morning will be fine. I will prepare lunch for your visit, so no need to worry about packing food." Cupping his hand to her face, he said, "My dear Adriena, thank you for keeping me posted. I shall see you tomorrow. I'm sending two of my men to see that you make it back safely."

"Thank you, Mr. Bonnaire, for your protection and your kindness."

"You're very welcome. Now I bid you au revoir."

Not wasting any time, they hurried back to the cabin with a nice escort.

Darien held Serenity tightly in his arms, whispering words of encouragement and love, kissing her. As he heard the door close, he said, "Sounds like they just made it in."

Not a moment too soon, Adriena knocked on their door.

"Serenity," Adriena said. "I need to speak to you both. It's urgent. I have a message from your father, Darien."

Replying to Adriena, he said, "Give us a minute or two and we'll be right out."

Quickly, they got dressed and joined them. Serenity said, "What's so urgent?"

Adriena replied, "Darien, I was asked to relay this message. We are to see your father in the late morning."

"Is that all my father had to say, Adriena?"

"Darien, he did say not to worry about lunch. My apologies, but I needed to tell you before morning."

His reply was, "Very well, and thank you for telling me. My father must have a plan for what I discussed with him when we last talked at home."

Adriena said, "And just what could that be?"

"We will wait until tomorrow. If he says to come there, then we can't discuss it, and for a good reason."

"We will abide by his wishes, Darien."

Each fell into their own restless sleep, wondering what the morning would bring. At dawn, Serenity was awakened by an incredible churning in her stomach and ran from their bedside.

Barely making it to the bathroom, she began heaving with nothing in her stomach, then broke into a cold sweat with her face turning white. She felt nauseated and sick.

Darien quickly ran to her side, worried. "What's wrong?"

"I don't know. I was fine, and then all of a sudden, I wasn't."

"Maybe it was something you ate last night?"

"Yes, of course, it could be." Then her thoughts began running back and she let out a gasp, startled by the thought. She looked at Darien with color draining from her already pale face.

"Oh no! Not now. This can't be happening!" she said.

Worried, Darien said, "What is it, Serenity? You're scaring the wits out of me."

She ran back to the room once the feeling subsided, with Darien right on her heels.

Serenity looked at his worried face after he closed the door. Cupping his face, she said, "Darien, sit down, please. I need you to listen carefully. Not one word until I'm finished." With worry on his face, he nodded his head without a word.

"My sweet Darien, two days after we married, my flow was to return and I assumed it was only a few days late. Now I know that wasn't the truth. Today confirmed what I thought."

Shocked and excited, all in one, he said, as he caressed her stomach, "You mean, I'm to be a father? Are you certain this is true?"

She shook her head, and in a whisper, she said, "I'm afraid so."

Pulling her close to him while she was almost in tears, he said, "Don't you worry. We will get through this, I promise you. Nothing and no one will harm you, the woman I love, or the child you bear. On this, you have my most solemn promise. We need to tell my father." She shook her head in denial, and he said, "We must. He can help us, and at this point is our only choice."

She felt soothed as he held her tightly. Then Adriena came running. Knocking on the door, she asked, "What's all the commotion? Are you okay?"

Darien spoke up to say, "We're fine and we'll be out in a bit."

"Very well, we will get breakfast going for us."

He looked at Serenity to say, "Do you wish to tell her now?"

"No, not now. I'm not ready."

"As you wish." He kissed her and looked her straight in the eyes as he said, "She will need to know, and very soon."

"Darien, I just need to collect my thoughts for the time being. I know she will not take this well."

Cupping her face and making her look at him, he said, "I promise you, it will be okay. I will see to it. I promise you." He kissed her. "Let's get you a cold press cloth for your face."

She nodded in reply.

She walked back toward the kitchen and then, at the smell of food, she moved faster to the restroom with Darien right behind her. Not able to hold it back, hoping the others did not hear, she just let it go.

Alysa walked into the kitchen after she saw Darien grabbing a linen cloth from the closet, and said, "Adriena? Is everything okay with Darien and your sister?"

"They're fine. Why do you ask?"

"Oh, I just saw Darien scrambling for a washcloth from the linen closet, that's all."

"He did what? Here, can you finish this. I need to see about my sister."

"Adriena, I sure hope everything's okay."

"Me too, Alysa," she said as she hurried to where Serenity was.

Pounding the door, Adriena said, "Serenity! Darien! Let me in! What's going on?"

Looking at Serenity he said, "She needs to know." He waited for her approval to open the door.

Then, as it eased, she sat on the seat and said in a whisper, "Let her in."

He opened the door slowly and Adriena hurried through, her face draining quickly as she saw Serenity. Brushing her hair back from her face she said, "What's wrong? Why are you in here? You were fine last night." The color drained from her face as she read her

91

sister very well. She responded, "Oh no!" as Serenity shook her head yes and was in tears. "Are you absolutely certain of this?"

In a whisper, she replied, "Yes."

Darien looked at Adriena and said, "Not a word until we talk with my father. The less that they know, the better we'll be."

All agreed not to say a word to the girls' parents.

After his wife had been in the bathroom for about an hour, Darien looked at Serenity and said, "Are you well enough to go back to the room, or would you like to try and eat something?"

"No food. Not right now. Yes, I'm okay. I'm going back to the room," Serenity replied.

Darien said, "I'll take her back."

Adriena said, "Is there anything I can get you?"

"Perhaps some water."

"I'll bring it to you."

Adriena went back to the kitchen to lend a hand.

"Is everything okay?"

"Yes of course, Alysa. Serenity will be fine. She just doesn't feel too good. She may be coming down with something, or it could have been something she ate. Darien is taking care of her."

"I sure hope she feels better soon, Adriena."

"Surely she will feel better in a day or two. I need to take her a glass of water. Perhaps some dill juice to help with nausea."

"You really think that will help her, Adriena?"

"I don't know, but my mother swears by it." She left to go see Serenity.

"Here, Serenity. Drink this first. It may ease your symptoms."

"Where did you get this and how did you come to know of it?"

"It's one of Mother's old remedies. Remember, Serenity?"

"I remember. I had forgotten. Thank you, and I need to rest for a bit, then get ready to go see Darien's father."

They went and ate while Serenity rested, prepared the horses after packing their belongings quickly and quietly into the satchels they'd brought in ready, and then hurried to Darien's father's house.

Chapter 15

Before the Storm

As she looked at her sister, Adriena said, "You must be feeling better. I can see the color has returned to your face."

"Mother's old remedy does help, tremendously."

Adriena smiled at her comment.

It only took them an hour to get to Darien's house. Markis welcomed them in. They headed to the family room while lunch was being prepared.

Darien began before his father and said, "Father, we must tell you something of grave importance."

"What is it, Son?"

"Serenity? Shall I tell him or will you?"

"You can, Darien."

"Father, she is with child, and I'll not have her father lay a hand on her. He must not know, especially now. Is there anything we can do? I wish to come back to my family, and God willing, to raise my son or daughter."

Markis looked at Serenity and replied, "Is this true?"

Serenity shook her head and said, "I'm afraid it is. Is there anything that can be done? I'll leave home if the need warrants it."

Markis replied, "I see. This changes things a bit. Son, I need you to fix up that place you went to. It is very well hidden. Take Adriena and Serenity with you so that they can learn it. Serenity, love, it will not be an easy transition for you, but this must be done. You will need to write a letter to your mother that must not be opened until you've left. You should wait until your father leaves, so he won't suspect it. Understood?"

"Yes, sir. I can do this."

"Your mother may mean well, and I believe she tries; nevertheless, she cannot be trusted. Believe me, I hate to say it. One day soon, I hope she will come around to do what is right, but for now, this must be done. I'll not take any chances with my first grandchild."

Serenity replied, "Is there anything else?"

"Darien? Shall we show them? They both will need to know if we are to succeed."

"Yes, Father." Noticing Serenity's uneasiness about what was going on, he comforted her by saying, "Don't worry. My father and I found a way to take care of you and your sister at least until the war is over. This will help you both stay safe if the need should ever arise. Besides, you will love what we are going to show you." As he said it, he nudged her gently.

"We should eat first. Besides, we will have plenty of time to take all of this in. Shall we?" Markis replied.

They went and ate. Darien said, "Serenity, seems your appetite has returned and you seem to be feeling better."

"Guess I needed to eat a little something, and yes, I'm feeling much better."

Adriena smiled as she replied, "Dill juice does wonders, doesn't it?"

Laughing a little at her comment, Serenity said, "Yes, I suppose it does."

"Good, then we shall make sure you get it every morning. Maybe we can keep Mother from noticing so soon."

Darien said, "You just need to keep it from your father until he leaves. Then leave a letter for your mother and leave before she sees it. Then you are both to come here, so we can learn all that is needed. Father, would you like to tell them the best part, or shall I?"

"Son, you seem to be doing a great job telling them, please continue."

"Very well." Turning to them, he said, "I've talked to Father, letting him know that you both would like to attend college. With everything that has come about, it is not safe going to college. He has a private tutor coming to train you both in the field of your study. I wish to be back before the baby arrives. Although I'm not able to promise it, I promise you I will do everything possible and try."

"Are you serious? I am to learn with my sister?" Serenity replied with excitement.

"Yes, my father has hired the one that will teach you everything there is needed to know. One more thing." He paused, then said, "Serenity, I can't stress enough that you must time the letter perfectly for this to work. You will know when. Adriena, make sure you get her here as quickly as possible. I want to see you both safe, and hope I can see that you are. I couldn't bear losing my sister or wife."

Markis responded, "When you reach the edge of our land, my men will see that you make it here safely. That I promise you."

Adriena and Serenity breathed a sigh of relief.

"Now, let me show you something wondrous, and this house is where it stands," Markis said with a smile as he led them.

Serenity gave Darien a look, wondering what was going on. Darien just smiled, taking her hand, leading them where they went.

Markis replied, "Watch your step as you enter. There are three ways in and out. One way is where Darien took you first, Serenity. This is another."

"And the last?" Adriena said.

"The last leads deep into the mountain, going through to the other side. Should you ever have to use it, on the other side you will have three accesses. One leading above ground, one heading to here, and one leading to an open access to a beautiful waterfall with the clearest waters I've ever seen. Take all of this in little by little and learn what you can as quickly as possible."

Adriena replied, "What about my sister, when her time draws near?"

"No need to worry, Adriena. The one that is to teach you and your sister is my trusted friend. He is our family physician and you will learn everything possible through him."

"You think of everything," Serenity replied.

"Serenity, I assure you we do our best to plan ahead, and it is good to finally have someone to share it with."

Serenity and Darien stayed with his father, helping each other to prepare before the weather changed. They learned more survival so that Serenity could adjust when Darien was called to duty. Adriena visited with Alysa, and both learned what was needed, until Alysa went to college. Adriena had chosen to stay due to the circumstances.

Day in and day out, they learned everything possible, from gathering food and water to knowing when they could go outside or stay put. Learning every inch of this place for three more weeks, they found new places to go, making it more accessible to the outside without being discovered. A perfect setting to live in if the need should ever arise. They worked with this until it was time to go home and face their mother once more.

Chapter 16

Unraveling Ties

On the way home, Adriena said to Serenity, "We need to find a way to keep Mother and Father from knowing you are with child. Especially before the war."

"How well do I know, Adriena. It is going to be so hard hiding this excitement as well as my sadness from our mother. You know I will do my best not to say a word."

"I know, Serenity. I also know how Mother can be. Let's just see what she says and counter it as best we can. Okay?"

She nodded in reply as they pulled up in the yard. They went ahead and took care of the carriage and horses so they could be done with that, giving more room for them to rest.

Excitedly, their mother greeted them at the door. "I'm so happy to see you girls finally making it home. I trust you girls enjoyed your time with your friend…oh, what is her name again?"

"Alysa, Mother," Adriena replied.

"Lovely girl." Not missing a beat, she added, "I trust you stayed away from that boy's family as your father requested."

Sarcastically, Serenity said, "Darien is his name, Mother. You knew of how I felt before we left."

"Yes, I suppose I did, but still I hoped you'd heed your father's warning. By the looks of it, and the tone of your voice, I would wager that you did not."

Adriena, taking the tension out of the air, or at least attempting to, said, "Speaking of Father, where is he now?"

"Truly sorry, but I'm afraid you girls just missed him. He will not return until that stupid war is finished. He did ask me to give you this message. He said to tell you both he loves you, and to be sure you help more around the keep."

"Did he now?" Serenity said sarcastically again. "He has no love for us. All he does and says is manipulative and controlling. Not once have we seen any show of compassion or love in his eyes."

"That's enough, Serenity. How dare you speak of your father in that way! What is the matter with you? You seem different. You've changed quite a bit. It's that boy! Darien, isn't it? I saw your last dance. You danced as your father and I once danced. I hope you did nothing foolish. Tell me you did not!" Noticing more of her daughter's features, she continued, "By the looks of your face, you're hiding something. I intend to find out." Her mother started again, saying, "You have changed." She paused while Serenity held her gaze, and then she continued, "That dance was a dance of secrets. The way you moved, you are definitely hiding something. Tell me now or I'll find out later. Just know, I will find out."

Thinking back to her own dance, Serenity's mother remembered and gasped at the thought of it. "Oh no, Serenity, please tell me you didn't. Please say it is not true."

Shaking from her head to toes, Serenity was having difficulty standing.

Adriena, speaking up on her behalf, said, "Mother, can't we rest a bit? It was a long ride."

"Adriena, I'll ask you once. Do not interfere. Now, Serenity, you have some explaining to do, young lady, so let's hear it!"

"I have nothing to say, Mother!"

"Oh, yes you do! You have plenty to say. I will start since you will not come away with the truth." Heatedly, she continued, "Tell me, Serenity. Have you lain with Darien?"

"Mother! That is none of your business!"

"On the contrary, I can see the glow in your face, and your eyes don't lie. Your father would be furious if he were here. What else have you done that I should know about!" Shaking Serenity for answers, she said, "Tell me! Tell me now!"

In tears, Serenity could no longer hold it in. Angered, she said, "Well, I'm glad he isn't! He's ruined everything we love and hold dear! I hate him! I swear, I hate him!"

Her mother slapped her for her tone, which she'd never done.

Serenity, in full tears, ran out the door. She didn't stop till she was well out of range and could not hear her mother calling, "Serenity, SERENITY, my daughter, come back! Come back…"

Adriena, glaring at her mother, said, "You are wrong, Mother! I had hoped just this once you would have taken our side, not Father's, and I was wrong to have ever believed you would. Know that we loved you both, but you should have been more in tune with how we've felt." She ran after Serenity, not even allowing her mother the opportunity to reply. Never seeing the pain that crossed her mother's face or the anguish that filled her tearing eyes.

Of course she loved her daughters, and she knew that Tomáš also loved them so very dearly. Perhaps he held too tightly. He was known to do that. Smother with his love that which he held most dear. Why couldn't the girls understand their complex father? Perhaps it was the many days of absence since these rumors of war had started again. War! That ugly word. He had seen so much devastation when he was young. One of the few to come out of the many battles without lasting physical injuries. But, oh, the injuries to his soul.

With the girls out of sight, she ruminated on how the war changed her loving, compassionate husband from a happy, easygoing fellow into a hardened and clearly suspicious man, focused on domination. It was that domination that led to his survival and his many subsequent promotions. But what worked with his men created a hurtful environment for his twin girls, and at times, an uncomfortable living situation for them all.

Finally catching up to her sister, Adriena said, "Serenity, it's okay. We knew it was coming and the fact is we have to face this. We need to go back and finish this. You need to write the letter tonight. We will put it on the table for her to see, and you must see Darien before he leaves. Being here is not good for you or the baby. Can you be strong enough to handle the rest that may be said?"

Shaking her head, she said, "I believe so. I will at least try."

"Serenity, when you write the letter, I wouldn't say anything about the baby if we can help it, all right? Only because we can't trust Mother, at all."

"Adriena, I will do what I can, and you know my words sometimes come before I think."

"I know you can do this. If it helps, look at me when you need to. Come on, let's go back before she sends a search party after us." This brought a halfhearted smile to Serenity's face, and, linking arms, they walked back.

"If we have to. At least it is only for the night."

As they walked in the door, they found their mother sitting in front of the fireplace. She looked up to say, as calmly as she could, "Serenity, understand you are not allowed to see him again. Your father has forbidden it."

"Mother, I am sorry, but I will not and cannot obey this order."

"So you will disgrace our family in this way? What are you thinking?"

"You think me stupid? I'll have you know, he is rightly my husband in every way! You know Father would have never allowed it, and I would gladly do it all over, the same as before. Yes, we married in secret and it is a binding that can never be broken. Tell me, Mother, would you begrudge me this small bit of happiness, just to have me endure all of Father's tactics and perhaps go mad in doing so?"

"I suppose, Serenity, when you put it that way, I would not begrudge you at all. Still, you could have come to me and let us discuss this."

"Now, Mother! Do you really believe I would even grace your presence after that stunt you just pulled? I think not!" Again, the angry words were out, and she took no notice of the wounded look in her mother's eyes.

"Serenity, I suppose you're right. Though you know your father will be furious as soon as he hears it."

"Please, Mother, I beg of you not to tell him. I will never forgive you if you do."

"Serenity, the only promise I can make is that I will try."

"Mother, I am tired of arguing, and I am exhausted from the trip. Will you please excuse me? I need to rest."

"I will allow you to be excused, but we are to discuss this tomorrow. I disagree and feel there is more to this, but I'll not say anything more. In time, I should hope you will find a way to tell me. I'll leave it up to you." Even as she spoke these words that she knew she must, her heart broke. "There is one thing I would like to know, Adriena. What is your reason in this, and what did you have to contribute? Never mind, we will discuss this tomorrow. Goodnight, girls. Try and get some sleep."

Without a word, they went to their room. With Adriena's help, Serenity wrote her letter. As tears trickled down her cheeks, she wished it could have been different and wondered if this rift in her heart would ever heal. Until now, she and her mother had always been close. Every confidence was shared, so why should this be so different? Yes, she had shut out her mom with the first lies. Now she was wondering if being truthful from the beginning would have been better.

She voiced those concerns, and Adriena assured her that, because of Father's influence, Mother couldn't have been included. This was the reason she had to be kept in the dark. Even so, Serenity knew that this letter would break her mother's heart and was loath to leave it for her.

The next morning, focusing on the trip to be made and wishing not to encounter their mother, the girls snuck out the door early. Serenity left the letter on the table and they hurried as fast as they could without the horses, lugging their bundled clothes, grateful that they hadn't yet unpacked. As promised, Darien's men were waiting for their arrival with the horses so they could ride the rest of the way.

Looking at Adriena, Serenity said, "I hope we're not too late."

Finally they made it to Darien's house. His father was waiting to greet them. They dismounted their horses, and he had hugs for both of the young women.

Markis said, "It's good to see you again. Though I would love to hear what happened, we must hurry. You need to see Darien before he is to leave. It won't be long before your father arrives."

"Do you know how long?" Serenity replied.

"Only that he is a few days away."

"Come, let's get you settled. Adriena, I wish for you to remain here and perhaps tell me what transpired at home. Serenity, Darien waits for you. Go where I showed you to go, and he will be there."

While Markis had one of his servants bring some refreshments, Adriena stayed inside the house, telling him everything that had transpired. Serenity went to the passage to meet Darien. Walking on a rocky path that smoothed to timeworn limestone beneath her feet. How fragrant each step as Serenity found the aroma coming from the rose petals being crushed underfoot with each step along the floor. Illuminating gems within the walls lit her way.

Darien was waiting just on the other side. As she stepped through, he was quick to cradle her in his arms. "I was so worried about you." Kissing her, he said, "Know you are safe here. I promise I will fight many." With Serenity's tears flowing again, he cradled her to comfort her.

"Sh. Sh. Sh. It's okay. We will one day find a way to make amends. You have my word on that, and I intend to keep it. Come, I want you to see this."

"What? Where are we going?"

"I need you to see the passage within the mountain. It only takes an hour to get there, and it is still early in the day." They went through cavern after cavern until they came to the last.

"Oh, wow! Darien, this is heavenly."

"I knew you'd love it. I need you to come here as a last resort. We will come to this place when this nightmare is over. Okay? Now, come, follow me."

"If you insist. Know I would like to test the waters below the waterfall one day."

"We shall, my love. We shall," he said as he kissed her hand. Leading her with his arm around her waist, he took her to another secluded place. Candlelight enhanced the natural glow in the walls surrounding them.

"When did you prepare this?" she said, looking at all the pillows and blankets surrounding them, with an arrangement of fruit on the side.

Smiling, he said, "When one of my father's men could see you coming, he raced back here to tell me."

"My fears are calmed by my lover's embrace, soothing the very depths of my soul. I shall remember until the day you return to me," she said, kissing him back.

He swung her up in his arms, then laid her beside him in the comforting caress of the blankets and pillows beneath them.

In a whisper, he said, "I will find a way to see our child born, somehow, some way. I don't want you to go through this alone. Promise you will be strong for me and our unborn child. Know that I love you immensely."

"I promise, Darien, to do my best and be strong."

As he made love to her before their return, he softly caressed every inch, exciting their love to the fullest height of ecstasy. As he held her in his embrace, they lay for several hours. Then returned to their own true home, awakening to morning's light. With a gentle caress, he kissed her deeply. Back to the world from whence they came, where they neither would like to be.

Chapter 17

Sudden Impact

Markis said, "Adriena! Quickly, now, I need you to go below! Find Darien and Serenity. Tell them to stay put. Under no circumstance are either of you to come out!"

"Why?"

"Adriena, it's your father! I don't have time to tell you. Please, hurry! He is here for my son, and I'm going to plead for more time to prepare. Now hurry, before he sees you."

Adriena ran to find the others. Just as she went through the entrance, she saw them heading her way. Running to them, she said, "No, we are to stay here. Darien, your father demanded we stay here till he says it's clear."

Tears streamed down Serenity's face as Darien said, "You know I wanted more time with you. I can't let my father take this brutality just because of me. I must go. I'm the one he wants."

Kissing her, he said, "I love you and I always will. I promise, I will find my way back to you."

"No, don't leave me, not now. I love you so much. I can't bear to lose you."

"Please, Serenity, don't make this harder than it already is." He kissed her once more and said, "Goodbye my love," in his language. He disappeared through the entrance, making his way as if to come in through the front door.

"Hey! What's going on! Leave my father be. He's done nothing wrong."

Commander Kozlov said, "He said you weren't here, yet here you stand."

"I wasn't here, so he didn't lie. What matters is I am here now," Darien replied.

"And are you ready as we had discussed before, Darien?"

"Yes, sir. If you wouldn't mind, I need a few minutes to grab my things."

"Very well, we will wait or you will leave without them."

"Understood, sir."

Markis said, "Please excuse me to help my son so you can be on your way."

"Very well, you may do so."

"Father?" Darien said. "Please tell her I love her. I will find my way back, or I will die trying."

"Darien, I will tell her everything, except the last of what you said." He hugged his son as he headed out the door and yelled after the departing pair:

"Kozlov! Take care of my son. He is all I have."

Kozlov nodded his head in reply.

Markis watched as his son disappeared into the shadows.

He turned to Serenity and Adriena and said, "Don't worry. I will take care of you until my son returns. It will be okay. You will see."

Arabel was frantic, not knowing where her daughters were. Not knowing where they'd gone was devastating. Though she was thankful for the words of love buried in the last letters, her heart was broken. She realized that an old friend of long ago might have a clue to the whereabouts of her daughters. She would seek the help of this old friend. But would he in turn help her? It had been years since they'd last spoken, and even though she knew that this was the only person who might know where her daughters had gone, what would be the first step in the process? The letters indicated that one of her daughters was in love and possibly with child. The betrayal of her love was a deep wound that she would never give up. She had hopes to reconcile from the last words spoken. With a plea from within her mind and shattered heart, she said, "Come hell or high water, I will not rest until I see my girls again, or…I will die trying."

Chapter 18

Boundaries

Their mother woke in the morning light. She made her way to the kitchen and noticed something strange on the table. She opened what looked to be a letter written in her daughter's hand. As she read, these words began:

"Mother, know that it pains me to write these words without any more discussion face to face." She dropped the letter on the table and ran upstairs. The treads screamed their anguish as her feet pounded on each step, and the banister groaned under the punishment of Arabel's grasp. Her heart thundered with fear as she checked their room. She let out a cry, and said aloud, "No! What have you done? Where did you go?" Then, calming down, her heart slowed and she gathered her thoughts and returned to the table. With streaming tears fogging her vision, Arabel prepared to read the rest of the letter...

"Mother, we both love you dearly and please don't worry. Just know we are safe and we will keep in touch as best we can. If you must write, give it to the one that delivers ours to you. Know this, we will not return home until it is safe to do so. I truly love Darien with all my heart and I will await his return. Adriena will stay for as long as I do. Know for now, we will keep in touch by letter."

Her thoughts were racing, wondering what now. "What am I to do? How am I to tell your father?" Arabel said to herself as she wrote them a letter, ready to send as instructed.

Meanwhile, back at Darien's home, Markis introduced the girls to the professor that would teach them about nursing. Serenity and Adriena were somewhat apprehensive about the lessons that would begin on the following day.

They worked every day as hard as they could, learning everything they could to be on the ready to assist the wounded as the war raged on. Not knowing what they would face if they were called on, they needed to learn quickly. Serenity hoped to be close to Darien if they were needed anytime soon. Both Markis and Adriena continued looking for a way to bring Darien home before Serenity's time drew near.

Markis kept the girls informed of Darien's position with the help of one of his men. Darien wrote as often as he could, giving them something to look forward to seeing.

After receiving a letter of worry from their mother, Adriena wrote back to tell her they were both in school and learning everything they could. She explained it would be difficult for them to write often. Adriena assured her not to worry.

After a month had gone by, Darien sent two letters by his father's messenger.

Markis walked through the door with a smile saying, "Serenity, this letter is addressed to you and the other to me. They are from Darien." He handed her the one, and she began shaking as she opened it nervously.

"My love, know that I love you and our unborn child more than life itself. I so long to be with you again and miss you immensely. I promise I will find a way and return to you before the birth of our child. I sent two letters now, because I don't know the time I will be allowed to send another. War is getting intense and your father is

110

demanding much more. I will need to make a huge decision your father has put upon me. I don't know that I can go through with it. He is clear of what his decision will be if I do not. Don't you worry, I will be fine through this. Know my father knows the situation, and he will do everything he can to help me. Rest assured he can do this. Please write to me so I can keep a good thought while I'm here. By now, my father should have read the letter I sent him, and I must go. They are calling me. Know I love you and I will see you again soon, my love. Darien."

Serenity waited patiently until Markis finished reading his letter in hopes he would tell her.

Markis was very careful as to what he revealed to her. He knew the burden of what it could do if she were to know everything. He didn't know how she would handle the whole truth should she find out.

Darien's letter to his father:

"Father, it is good to send you this letter. I know I told Serenity some of what is going on, but not everything. If it weren't for our unborn child, I would ask you to tell her. If she should ever come across this or even read it, know this is the only reason I do not. This is only for the safety of Serenity. Now, Father, I am troubled. Though I love her father, he has asked me to get rid of everyone in that village we are to besiege. The reason I cannot do this is there are widespread innocents among them. I believe we can save them. If I do as he has demanded, I'll remain his first command. If I should not do this, he will give me a lashing for punishment, throwing me in the brig. This can take months to recover from. Although I am prepared to take this, I am not sure which way to turn. My heart says I should not. My will says I should but not without cost. The images would haunt my dreams and possibly make me go mad. One pain is less than the other and I will follow my heart to the path I should take. Know that if I should do this, there's no way to tell when my next letter will be. I ask you to tell Adriena, but do not tell Serenity, unless a time comes that she should know. Wait for the time to pass for the least amount of danger to her and our unborn child. If she should by chance have this child while I am away, I ask her to name it after my love if it is a girl. If it is a boy, ask her to name him what she deems worthy. I know I will love whatever is chosen, because it is a part of her and me. If you can write in time before this takes place, I should welcome your thoughts on what is at hand. I must bid you adieu, my time for this letter is at an end. Love, your son, Darien."

Serenity quickly wrote her letter to Darien and sent a poem of her thoughts. While she was writing, Markis had Adriena read what Darien had sent. Then Serenity, after handing the letter to Markis to be sent, went to the special place where she'd last spent time with Darien.

"Adriena," Markis said. "Will you please go check on Serenity? I know this is a very difficult time for her. As long as you both are under my care, I'll not let anything happen to either of you."

"Yes, sir, I will check on my sister." She walked to where Serenity was, not knowing exactly the state of mind she was in.

As she neared her presence, she heard the song of "A Beloved's Cry." Serenity sang of her love's embrace.

Needing peace, for war's own sake
My thoughts of you, I lie awake
Longing for my love's embrace
No matter the cost we face

Away from all this treachery
In my dreams, you carry me
Hoping that it won't be long
For you I weep, yet I'll be strong
Patiently, I wait and sigh
Hear, my love, a beloved's cry

112

Just to feel your fiery kiss
Know it's you I terribly miss
Warm embrace, I feel and see
Find your way, come back to me

Let me know it won't be long
For you I weep, yet I'll be strong
Patiently, I'll wait and sigh
Hear, my love, a beloved's cry

Whether this be a girl or boy
Know my life, it's filled with joy
Longing for your touch be real
My love I wait, so I can feel

Tell me that it won't be long
So I'll not weep and make me strong
Never say the words goodbye
Hear, my love, a beloved's cry

Quiver my soul and make me quake
To feel your love before I wake
Longing for your love and touch
Your warm embrace I feel so much

Drawing near a winter's chill
Sun is high, and time be still
Our love is strong, we'll not deny
Hear, my love, a beloved's cry

Serenity sat in a place where they'd once been together. As she sang the last lines, she broke down and buried her face in the pillows, not able to utter another word.

Adriena saw the pain her sister was in, and she ran to her side. Prompting Serenity to lay her head on her shoulder, Adriena said, "I'm so sorry you have to go through this. If there was anything I could do, I'd do it for you."

Between sobs, Serenity said, "There's one thing you can do. I need you to be honest with me. You can tell me what Father is doing to Darien. I know you read the letter sent to his father."

Adriena shook her head. "I must not say anything. I was told not to for your sake."

"Come on, Adriena, I need to know. Now or later makes no difference to me, but I should find out now rather than later. I, too, know how Father is, and I need to have an understanding of what could transpire…"

Markis came out of the shadows and said, "Go ahead, Adriena, I can tell there's no holding anything from either of you."

"As you wish," she replied to Markis, then turned to Serenity. "First, I need you to understand we will do everything we can before this happens." She paused, letting that sink in.

"Adriena, forgive me, but please get to the point. I need to know now."

"Yes, of course," Adriena replied. "Father said Darien will be reprimanded if he does not follow his orders. Darien knows in his heart not to take that course and I'm sure he will not. You know his heart better than any of us."

Markis stepped over and handed her his letter. "I can see there is no keeping this from you. Just know we wanted to do what's best for you and the baby. Please forgive me for even thinking of withholding this information. I'm starting to believe it's better for you to know than to withhold anything from you. I just want you and my unborn grandchild safe and unharmed. You know I will do my best to help you anyway I can."

"Please leave me be. I wish to be alone for a little while. I promise I will be okay. Adriena, please, I wish for you to go. I won't be too terribly long. I just need a moment."

Both nodded against their own wishes. Reluctantly, they said, "As you wish, my lady." They went back to the house.

Whispering to herself, she said, "Darien. Please, come back to me. I need you now, my love." She held a pillow with a hint of his scent that faintly remained. She lay back, her eyes full of tears. Exhausted from the anguish, she fell asleep. Three hours later, Adriena was trying to wake her.

As her sister called, Serenity stirred, opening her eyes.

"Oh, thank heaven! You just fell asleep! Come on, let's get back to the house before he sends someone to get you."

"How long was I asleep? I must have lost track of time when I closed my eyes."

"Serenity, you've been here for three hours."

"Oh dear, I must have been exhausted. Let's quickly return to the house."

Adriena caressed her face, full of concern, and said, "You were exhausted because your thoughts are of Darien. I know you miss him tremendously. We need to find you some way to get your mind off of him, even if it is temporary."

"My apologies, but I just can't stop thinking about him, no matter what I do. I need to find a way to get him back to me. There has to be a way, Adriena! Please tell me you will help me!"

Hugging her sister for comfort, she said, "You know I will do everything I can to help. You have my word on it." Taking the tissue handed to her, Serenity wiped the tears from her eyes as they returned to the house. "I wish Mom would listen and be here for us. It would be so much better." Just as they neared the entrance, one of Markis's men stopped them from going through. Then they heard a familiar voice. Serenity looked at Adriena. In a whisper she said, "That's Mom! What is she doing here?" Adriena shrugged her shoulders, saying she didn't know.

"Serenity, let's listen. Maybe we can hear what they are saying."

"What are you doing here, Arabel? You shouldn't be here. Tomáš would not be happy to learn you came here, now, would he?"

"Please, Markis, I need to know the whereabouts of my girls! Serenity is in love with your son, and that gives me reason to believe you, and suggests you know where they are!"

"I am sorry, Arabel, but I cannot and will not disclose any information, with good reason."

"Markis, please, I beg of you to let me see them."

"I cannot, and it pains me to tell you so. I will, however, give consideration to possibly arranging a meeting with them. Mind you, don't get your hopes up. I will still need to talk it over with your daughters. They have to approve of this arrangement. Only then can I allow this to take place. Take it or leave it."

"Can you please see to it and make it happen? I need to talk to them and to tell them in person what their father asked me to tell them. It is urgent I get this message to them."

"Arabel, I make no promises. I can promise I will try. It is out of my hands otherwise."

"If you would be so kind, I would very much appreciate it. I need to find my way back home. I shall wait for your reply, and thank you for at least trying. Desperate times calls for desperate measures in keeping your family together, and I intend to do whatever I possibly can to make that happen."

"I'll consider your words. Please allow my men to escort you safely home. You shouldn't be alone in these parts, daylight or dark. Oh, one more question before you go, Arabel. Did, by chance, Tomáš leave any men to protect you while he is gone?"

"No! Should I have concern in need of protection?"

"Arabel, I only say this: if I were him, I would have made sure of it for my family's safety. If you would allow it, I will expand my men to your lands for protection. I only need your consent in doing so." He extended a piece of paper to read over and sign. "Please, read over what I offer. I do this for the girls, not for myself. You have much to discuss, and if possible, to heal wounds of all that has been thrust upon you. Please, Arabel, I wish for you to think about it, and consider my intentions behind it. You once knew me as well as my friend Tomáš. So much has changed, and I should hope that he is still my friend."

"Markis, I will look this over and consider your words carefully. Somehow, I have a feeling you are watching over my girls, and for that I thank you. Please, if you see them, will you let them know how much I do love them and that I am so sorry how this has come about."

"If I see them, I will certainly tell them, Arabel."

Arabel accepted the escort home.

After their mother left, Markis motioned for them to come into the house, saying, "I need you both to consider talking with your mother. Will you do this?"

Replying together, they said, "Yes, we will, this one time."

"Very well, I will send one of my men to arrange the meeting. Serenity, since you decided to let your mother know you are married, she needs to know about the child. I will leave that for you to discuss. Be prepared to answer what she asks. Know this will not be easy for either of you, and now it must be dealt with. I need you to consider carefully how you will handle this. Now, after we depart, I need you and Adriena to discuss what your next move will be, is this understood?"

"Yes, sir," they replied together.

"One more thing. There are some things you should know about your father. I had hoped your mother would have told you by now, but I can see she has not. I will discuss this with your mother when your meeting is to take place. I wish for her to tell you first. Know that if she does not, I will do what I must. I hope you will heed everything I tell you."

Serenity said, "I understand what I must do." She looked at her sister, and, with her approval, said, "My sister and I understand, and we will do as you ask." Adriena nodded as Serenity spoke.

"Good, I shall hold you to your word," Markis replied with a slight smile.

Chapter 19

Tides of Change

Tomáš said, "Darien, the time is almost here, and I need your answer in what we discussed. You have one month, and I'll await your reply. Is this understood?"

"Yes, sir. Understood, sir. Might I speak freely, sir?"

"Very well, because of your father I will allow it. This one time, Darien. Be quick with your words."

"Yes, sir." Hesitating a little as he spoke, he said, "Sir, there are many innocent people in that village."

"And your point is?" Kozlov replied.

"Sir, permission to try and save them, please. They don't deserve this end!"

"Darien, am I to understand your hesitation?"

"Sir, please let me try. I know of a way, and it will not jeopardize your efforts in the war. Let them see you have compassion. I beg of you, sir! Please!"

"Darien, I will say this only once. Only because you are the son of the man who once was my closest friend. Those families are raising their families to hate and to fight for their own cause as young as nine years of age. Tell me, what good will it do if we were to save even just one who has turned against us?"

"But, sir, some of them are innocent. Why make them guilty before they have lived? I believe in change, and that they can change. Please give them a chance!"

"Darien, I say this, and it is not to be taken lightly, as this comes from above my command. Now, for this reason, I will not go back on the command I was given, therefore, you will heed my words and consider what you must do. Do it not and you will face the consequences thrust upon you, son or no son of Markis. Do you understand these words clearly?"

Sadly, nodding in reply, he said quietly, "Yes, sir."

Tomáš put his hand to his ear, prompting him to speak louder.

Darien raised his voice without hesitation, boldly saying, "Yes, sir!"

"Now return to your post until I give the order and signal, Darien!"

Without another word, he returned to his post in anguish. Darien sent word to his father of what had transpired. He rounded up some trusted men and saved as many as they could before they began to lay siege to the village. His father's men took them to another place to keep them hidden from Kozlov's wrath. It took a month to save a few villagers at a time. Darien was about to attempt another, until his commander called him in to talk with him.

"Darien, do you know why I called you here?"

"No, sir." Darien stood waiting to hear what he had to say.

"Darien, I have come to learn that some people in those villages have been aided in a rescue attempt." As he pointed at a map, he said, "One of my men tells me you are one that has been aiding them. I should shudder at the thought that you had anything to do with this. Now, I am only going to ask you once: did you or did you not have anything to do with this? I must warn you, tell me the truth and I will lessen the severity of your punishment. Know that if you do not, you will suffer far greater. Now, what is to be your reply?"

Swallowing hard, he looked at his commander and said, "Yes, sir, I did and I am not sorry. I deeply felt they needed a chance."

"Am I to understand you went against my wishes defiantly?"

"Yes, sir," he said while hanging his head down. "Please, sir, permission to speak freely?"

"I will permit it. Know that I will follow through with punishment. Now what is it?"

"Sir, my father told me you once wanted to help others and you showed great compassion toward them. Please, I beg you to turn the tides and change it."

"Darien, times have changed and I will not waver on my command. Now, prepare for your punishment. I want you to really think about your decisions."

Reluctantly, he replied with a nod. Noticing the angered look in his commander's eyes, he felt at that moment he had truly crossed the line and now feared what was to happen.

"Darien, I will not allow my emotions to ever again cloud my judgment in the decisions I make. I was foolish to have ever done so and I will not allow myself to be put in this situation again. Now, my men will escort you to holding cell in the mountain, and there you will wait for your punishment to begin. I am truly sorry I have to do this, but I cannot and I will not allow this to go unpunished. Now go and await your fate. I should hope that you will learn your lesson after this is over. You will follow my command or you will suffer this fate, am I clear?"

Afraid to say anything more, his only reply was, "Yes, sir!"

Kozlov's men escorted him to the holding cell to wait for his punishment, along with others that had participated.

Darien wrote a letter to his father in hopes that he could persuade his father to find a way and help him. As he told his father of his fate, bringing tears to his own eyes, he pled for a way to come home. He sent his father these words:

"Father, I fear that I am risking much to send you this letter. My hopes are for you to see this letter in time. Please, Father, if there is anything you can do, I need you now! I am sending this letter by one of your trusted friends. Serenity's mother may know of a way. Please, talk to her. Tell my love I love her and our love that is on the way more than life itself. Know that I would do anything I possibly can to make my way back to her, now and always. Love, Darien."

Chapter 20

Unwinding Ties

Markis sent a letter by one of his men to Arabel, asking her to meet him in his home, with explicit instructions orchestrated through her daughters. She was to be here at noon on the first day of the week. It had been two and a half months since she'd last seen them.

At noon the next day, Arabel was there, anxious and saddened at the same time to see her daughters.

Markis opened the door after the knock, and standing in front of him was Arabel. "It's nice to see you again, Arabel, although under better circumstances would have been nice. Here are the girls, as promised, and at your request. They asked to see you. Arabel. There is one request I ask of you and I will hold you to your word. Please do not disclose anything discussed here. Not a word to Tomáš or to any of his men. Do I have your word on this? Know that if my ears learn that you've done anything to jeopardize my wishes, you will never be allowed to set foot on my lands again. The girls wish you to be a part of their lives, and until my son is home, it will be at a cost."

"Yes, of course, Markis, please let me see my daughters."

"Arabel, I should like to ask you one more thing. May I?"

"What is it, Markis?"

"Your daughters do not know our history and I wished to tell them. I would like your permission, if I may have it, or let it come from you. Just know that I will tell them should I have need to. You know in your heart I would never steer them wrong. I've no influence at all in their decisions."

Giving in to his request, she said, "Yes, Markis, you have my permission, though I would love to be here and help you tell it."

"Very well, Arabel, this will be your daughters' decision. Let us have lunch before any discussions, shall we?"

Half smiling, she agreed, and then she saw her daughters. Not knowing exactly what to say, these words came to the surface: "It does my heart good to see my girls." As she looked at Markis, she said, "I see you have been taking great care of them, and I thank you for that."

Adriena and Serenity walked toward their mother as she opened her arms to embrace them. They accepted the embrace with caution.

Adriena broke the tension. "It is good to see you again, Mother. We've missed you and have much to discuss, but all in due time. Mother, don't expect everything all at once."

"Yes, dear, I will listen. It does me good to see both of you, and I've missed you terribly." Tears flowed freely among all the women as the reunion began to melt the hardened hearts.

Markis broke up the reunion, saying, "A fine meal is prepared and waiting on our arrival. I would like to eat while it is still warm. There is plenty of time in the day to see each other. Shall we go and enjoy?"

Arabel, wiping the tears from her eyes as Markis handed her a tissue, replied, "Yes, of course, Markis. I mean it, thank you."

Smiling with a nodding gesture, he guided them to their places at the long kitchen table where bread, meat, and drink were set out on wooden serving platters The rustle of the light-green tablecloth was the only sound as the group sat in and proceeded to pull up the rough-hewn upholstered chairs. For a few minutes, silence sounded louder than any words, as each person was deep in thought as they helped themselves and satisfied the hunger that had started to make itself known.

Not a word was spoken as they finished their meal and retreated to the family room for discussion. Serenity had a slight shuffle to her step due to her growing pregnancy. Not enough yet to really be noticeable…except perhaps to a practiced eye.

Serenity looked at her sister as she broke the silence, saying, "Mother, what I must tell you goes no further than this room, and please permit me to finish before you say anything. Can I have your word on this? I mean this sincerely, that if this trust is broken I will not say a word again in confidence. I know this may seem harsh, but I ask for this secrecy for a reason. Now, do I have your promise?"

Reluctantly, abiding by their wishes, her mother agreed to these terms. "Yes, Serenity, you have my promise."

Markis nodded his head in approval.

Serenity began, "Very well. First of all, dear Mother, I have missed you greatly. What I am about to tell you must not be uttered outside these walls." After letting that sink in, she continued, "Mother, I want you to understand, I love Darien from the depths of my soul. Considering the times we are facing, we chose the most difficult path. You know well of Father's intentions, and he would have never agreed to this. For that reason, we married in secret. This is the unbreakable vow that cannot be undone. Adriena, being of rightful age to consent, doing this willingly, without hesitation helped make this happen. I'm not asking for your approval, though I would love to have it. Instead, I wish for you to be happy for us."

Mother responded, "I can see, Serenity, how much you do love him. I have a confession to tell you girls." She looked at Markis as she said this. "Girls, I was an only child to my parents. I too shared the same feelings, but it was not with your father. You see, my father forbade it, and I was not permitted to do as you did. It gives me great joy you followed your heart, but at the same time gives me pain of my own."

Serenity's eyes began to fill with tears as her mother continued.

"What I am about to tell you, your father would be furious to know I told you. Before you were born, Markis and your father were best friends. The person I fell in love with is sitting right next to you."

Shocked gasps sounded as they continued to listen, while Markis sighed in relief that this years-long burden was being lifted from him as Arabel finally told them. He has been harboring this secret for too long. The first time he'd seen the twins, he was amazed at their likeness to Arabel. Of course he loved his wife, but it just wasn't the same. Perhaps the first love was just special… These thoughts flashed through his mind, here now, then gone. He shook his head to clear it, and then focused on what was being said.

"What you don't know is I loved Markis more than your father. My father would not hear of it, nor would he listen, therefore he forced an arranged marriage on me to marry Tomáš. He would not give me a reason and I had no choice at the time. Why he didn't approve of Markis, I do not know. I hated the arrangement and had to adjust to the marriage. Obviously, I did not love your father in the beginning but I grew to love him in a different way. I do not regret the love I had for Markis, though my choice was not allowed in my father's family tradition.

Although, after the first war, your father almost went mad. Markis took Tomáš to help him recover. Then when you girls came along, Tomáš returned to me from being under the care of Markis. I am afraid this war may take him from me again, if it hasn't already. My fear is that he may not be able to recover."

Looking toward Markis, she said, "I am sorry I did not tell them a long time ago. My feelings for you are the same, but my heart belongs to Tomáš. Please forgive me for not bringing this out earlier."

"Arabel, there is nothing to forgive." Markis reached for her hand and gave a light squeeze. "Know I will do what I must to bring my son home again. Remember, I saw the commander's brutal tactics firsthand, and I will not subject my son to this same fate. I have more reason now than before. I will leave it at that. Just rest assured that we are close friends and that never changes."

Adriena and Serenity were left speechless while Markis and their mother spoke. An awful nausea overcame Serenity and brought her back to the present. "I'm not feeling well and I need to be excused. Please, come back, and perhaps we can talk again. I'm sorry that I cannot stay."

Speaking to her mother, Adriena said, "I too must go. Know it was good to see you again. We do love you so very much, Mother. This seems to be a step in the right direction. I hope we can continue down this redeeming path." The emotions welled in the throats of the sisters, who choked back tears. Tears of hope, love, and foreboding. They hugged her one last time before leaving the room.

Exhausted, Serenity went to Darien's room, which was hers to use while he was away. Feeling nauseated, she lay down. Adriena fixed her some dill juice, saying, "Remember to drink it slowly." Serenity drank, but it did not make her feel better this time. Adriena got a warm washcloth and put it on her forehead, and stayed to make sure her sister would be okay.

Arabel lingered to catch up on a few things. She turned to Markis to say, "Markis, my girls seemed to be different, especially Serenity. There is a blossoming about her. What can you tell me?"

"Arabel, I'm truly sorry, I can't say a word without their approval. Serenity needs to be the one. You know I would do anything for you and for your girls. I will take great care of them, I promise. All I did was give them a safe place to be. I, too, know how Tomáš is, and I will find a way to bring my only son home."

"I will try to understand, Markis. I, too, wish for my daughters to come home. Both of our children are estranged from us. My girls due to misunderstandings, your son due to war."

"Arabel, if I had my choice I would ask you to stay here while Tomáš is at war, just to keep you safe. I fear greatly that Tomáš has changed already for the worse. Believe me, I hope I'm wrong, but I have reason to believe otherwise. You know, with my rank, I cannot go into details. There are things I see that you cannot even imagine to see. Just know my home is open, should you ever change your mind. If anything, it might even bring you closer to your own daughters. Please think about my offer."

"Markis, I will think on your kind offer. It is more than I could have expected. You know this is not an easy decision for me to make. I, too, will do anything for my daughters, by taking things slowly and listening closely."

Markis said, "Arabel, I will talk to your daughters and see if we can come to an agreement. I make no promises, but I will try for you. I know how painful this must be for you, and I see how it pains them as well."

"Thank you, Markis, and please send my love to them. I will wait for our next meeting. Till then, I shall write back until I can see them again." With that, Arabel left the room, found her cloak, and exited to her waiting carriage. The drive home would be longer than the drive here, which had been filled with jubilant and at times apprehensive exhilaration. The morning sun had stood high on the horizon, and now the shadows of evening were drifting into the forest, which seemed gloomier somehow… "What shall I do?" she thought. "Is Serenity expecting a child? How could that be? The signs were all there…"

Her mind was in turmoil as she guided the horses along the narrow roadway, which seemed to close in on top of her with the fading daylight. "Drat these woods," thought Arabel. She always preferred the open meadows. Where one could see the sky and the clouds, and the miles of open grasslands, where deer liked to graze. In the grasslands, the sun would warm one's back while one drove a carriage, and the breeze would cause the grass to roll like the waves of the legendary sea.

After Adriena checked on Serenity, being sure to cover her with a light blanket, she came back down the stairs. She came into the family room and surveyed the area…empty except for Markis. "Where's Mom? I was going to talk to her for just a bit."

"Adriena, your mother returned home and waits for you and Serenity to ask her to come back. I need you to talk to Serenity. I leave this decision for her to make, and her mind isn't as clear as it should be right now. I wish for Serenity to share the news of the baby to your mother so she knows she has a grandchild on the way." While Adriena was frowning and shaking her head no, he said, "Hear me out. It is not safe for your mother to be at home alone. I have asked her to consider coming here––at least until the war is over. You know I have the safest places to go on my land. My reason for this is, I fear your father may drive this war to his home because of his state of mind. I need to see if both of you can convince your mother to come here for her own safety."

Reluctantly, Adriena listened and decided to talk with her sister. "Mr. Bonnaire, I am worried about my sister. She went upstairs feeling nauseated, but none of the remedies I gave her are working, and she is so restless and cannot sleep. I know this cannot be good for her or the baby."

"I will send for our physician to check on her immediately. Let's not worry, okay?"

Markis did not waste any time. A messenger was immediately dispatched to bring their physician, Dr. Strombalini. Only a short time later, the good doctor appeared. He and his son Trevian came to a quick stop, their mounts still quivering from the exertion of traversing the uneven terrain, as they had come across the open property in avoidance of the road through the woods. The less attention they drew to this house the better. Prying eyes were everywhere these days, so the circuitous route through the meadow and up the dry creek bed and back through the woods was the best route. If followed, it would be quite evident. Dr. Strombalini had been a loyal family friend as well as physician since the family had settled in this region. The good doctor checked Serenity very carefully––everything he could think of was covered. Finally they left the room to meet Adriena's worried eyes. Adriena said in a worried tone, "Is my sister going to be okay? What's wrong with her?"

Trevian, who was training to be a doctor, looked at her, laying a hand on her shoulder, and said, "She needs lots of rest. Being away from Darien is causing her a tremendous amount of stress. Because she is not resting at night, it is causing her to have nausea." Then he looked at Markis and said, "The only thing that makes sense is to find a way to get Darien here as fast as you can. The quicker you have him here out of the war, the better off she will be. She is almost through her first trimester and it is crucial she doesn't have stress. Now we need to find a way to help her rest easy at night."

Markis said, "This definitely changes things. Your mother needs to know."

Adriena replied, "If she is able to rest, will this help most of it?" She was sure hoping so! They were twins after all, and even though Adriena wasn't getting violently ill like Serenity, her tummy still would be squeamish, and she could feel a draw on her own strength as Serenity's failed.

Trevian looked at this beautiful woman in front of him and said, "I believe this will help her very much." He handed Adriena some ingredients, saying, "Here, fix her some warm tea and add this to it. I believe it will be a tremendous help. Let's try it for a week and see how she does, okay?"

In a curious manner, feeling a signal radiating through him, she said, "Thank you, Trevian. I sure hope this will help her. Will you be coming to check on her again soon?"

"Sure, I can. That is, if my father doesn't mind." A knowing glance passed between father and son.

"Yes, Trevian, I think that is a good idea. Seems like these young ladies have lots to work through, so checking in on them would be right. Since you're at the point in your training where you would go solo, this seems like the right place to start. There are so many other patients that desperately need my attention. You'll do a great job––if you can keep this patient in line. Good luck, she seems quite determined, and with her mind churning day and night with real or imagined worries for Darien, she does need someone to check in on her. We don't want that baby coming before it has a decent chance of survival. That might be a good thing to remind her of…" Strombalini looked at his son. "I believe you are ready."

With a smile, Trevian looked at Adriena and said, "Looks like I will see you tomorrow."

They left, and as instructed, Adriena gave her sister this specially made tea, and stayed by her side as they rested for the night. Markis peeked in on the girls, and laid a blanket over Adriena as she lay by her sister.

Serenity had slept soundly all night, so soundly that, as the streaming sun woke her, she needed a few minutes to remember where she was and what had happened. So many things in such a short time. How could she possibly manage without Darien? Where was he? How was he? The letter had been so ominous, and as her thoughts started cascading over her, it seemed as if the sun started fading. Yes, it had been a surprise to get together with her mother again. She had steeled herself for the meeting, but was that wrong? She loved her mother and knew that her mother loved her too. So why was it that she hardened every time they encountered each

131

other? Those thoughts aside, Serenity felt a little better. She started for the restroom without help, and Adriena was startled by the movement. Adriena walked to the door and said, "If you need me, I'm right here."

Serenity replied, "I'm okay for now." A few minutes later, she returned to lie back down to continue the musings that were rattling around in her head. Before she could get her thoughts in check, Adriena asked her, "Are you hungry? Is there anything I can get you? Oh, and Trevian will be here before too long to check on you."

"Who's Trevian? Yes, I'm a little hungry."

"He is Doctor Strombalini's son. He is almost ready to be a doctor, following in his father's footsteps."

Noticing her sister's face as she talked about him, Serenity said with a smile, "You like him, don't you?"

Adriena smiled as she said, "He is very nice and not to mention very cute!" A slight blush crept up her cheeks, and her eyes seemed livelier than even this fresh morning sun could induce.

With a smile, Serenity said, "Adriena, it does my heart good to see you happy. Promise me you will see this through?"

"Serenity, I promise I will try. Honestly, I don't have a clue whether he likes me or not. All I can say is I felt a connection. At least your color has returned. You're not that pale, pale white from last night. It was a bit of a scare for me"

"Adriena, I must get this letter to Mom. I've waited long enough to send it."

"Might I inquire what you wrote to her, Serenity?"

"She needs to know this, Adriena, if she intends to keep coming here, and I decided this is the right time for me to say what is needed. Here is what I said to her. 'My Dear Mother...'"

"Oh dear, this doesn't sound promising," thought Adriena.

"I know you stayed in contact with Father. This will be said once. You knew and know how much I love Darien. I will never forgive either of you if Father lays a hand on him or if Father does not release him to come home. I will have a father that loves his child unconditionally. Know that if he does not come back to me, you will not be able to see me, my sister, or your grandchild when it arrives! I love you both dearly, but this will be hard to forgive should it come to pass. Think about that before you utter those words to Father. Know it gives me great joy to see you, but I can't continue to handle this pain. It is becoming unbearable. I need resolution, strength, and above all, to see my Darien again. This may be much to ask for, but these are my terms. If he can't find his way back to me, I will go to him. One way or another, I will see him. Adriena knows my heart and she knows I will do this. Either I have your help or I will go against your wishes no matter the consequence. It pains me to say this, but you know I must do this. Please send me the reply I need to hear, Mother. Love, your daughter, Serenity."

"Oh, Serenity, please don't send this to Mother. Let us find another way. There has to be another! I hear the pain in your voice, but think of the pain you are causing Mother. Do you really believe that she has or could have sway over what Father orders for his men? During these difficult times we should be pulling together. Mother needs us, just as we need her. Didn't you feel the love and the strength she brought into the room yesterday?"

Shaking her head, Serenity said, "No, Adriena. You know this must be done. I need to do this. Somehow, I must find my way to him, and before I am unable to travel. He is two days' ride from here, and I will go to him. I believe Mother can do something, and I've heard enough of her refusal. I need her to at least TRY and help me."

"You would risk the safety of your unborn child. Tell me, what will this accomplish, Serenity? Please give me a chance to come up with something less dangerous for you. Is there nothing I can say to convince you to change your mind?" She paused for a few minutes, deep in thought, then began again. "Wait a minute, I may have an idea. Will you give me a chance to see this through and fill you in on the details?"

"How long must I wait, Adriena?"

"Give me a couple of days, this might just work. There are a few things I must try to work on. I should know in a few days what we can do. First, I'm sending your letter. I want to see Mother's response. How about this: give me one week to see what this will do. The answer may be right under our nose."

"Adriena, I wish you would just tell me. Though I don't like this, I will wait for one week." With sternness in her voice and determination flashing in her eyes, she said, "I mean it! Only one week or I will do what I must."

Adriena hugged her sister and said, "I promise, Serenity. I will tell you as soon as I know, within a week."

Chapter 21

Silent Prayer

The beautiful warm sunshine had lasted only two days, and now for the last two days, a dreary drizzling rain had set in. Everything was gray and dripping, the trees, shrubs, roofs, bringing gratitude into the heart of Serenity as she rested in front of the flashing and flickering fire. In the silent prayer of her heart she began to ache for her love. The slight smell of the oak wood burning was somehow reassuring when compared to the drippy, cold, gray outdoors. Oh, how was her love faring in this ugly weather? Was he in a cold tent, or did he have a solid roof or cave to keep him warm and dry? She dearly hoped so. Her musings this morning were suddenly interrupted as Serenity jumped up out of bed with a sudden jolt of nausea. While running to the bathroom, she was sure she'd woken her sister, who was sleeping in the large bed just across from her. An hour later, she grabbed a warm washcloth to wash her face, and then headed back to the room.

Adriena, finally awake, hurried down the stairs to fix a drink in hopes to calm Serenity's nausea.

After nearly tripping as she hurried up the stairs, Adriena was relieved to see a bit of color in Serenity's face. "Adriena, please don't mention the word 'food' until this subsides," chided Serenity with a flicker of a smile.

Adriena chuckled as she said, "Not one word on it."

Just then, a knock on the door announced a breakfast tray. Markis had had a servant bring up a variety tray. Adriena answered, saying, "Thank you," while he put it on the table under the large window. "Ugh! I can't," moaned Serenity as she dashed for the bathroom door.

"Just have your breakfast, Adriena. I'll recover in here. Just save a dry piece of toast for me." Then she disappeared behind the bathroom door, where running water and heaving sounds could be heard.

"Are you okay? Can I get anything for you?"

"No, Adriena. I'll be fine. It has almost passed, and then the toast will be good."

Markis got a letter from Arabel letting them know she would be there for lunch. Adriena went downstairs to fix another drink for Serenity. Leaving her sister with the tea and the dry toast, she carried the tray with breakfast remains to the kitchen. After she did this, the wonderful aroma of fresh cinnamon rolls drew her into the kitchen, where she gratefully sat down next to Markis to share in a breakfast of fresh eggs and those glorious rolls. Adriena felt guilty as she devoured the delightful meal. She was ravenous. Not just now but at every meal. It seemed that she was eating for two! Poor Serenity was sick as a dog for most mealtimes, and had absolutely no appetite, yet here was Adriena with the appetite of a growing boy! She would have to tone it down or she would also look pregnant, only without the benefits of a sweet baby to come. This made her giggle, and the guiltiness faded away as she pictured herself as a fat lady. While sitting there eating, Markis noticed and said, "Is she sick again?"

Adriena, shaking her head in response, said, "Yes, and I believe it is just morning sickness this time."

"Nonetheless, I will send for Trevian and have him take a look at her before your mother arrives, just to be sure that is all it is."

"Yes, sir," Adriena replied.

She returned to Serenity after she ate. No sooner had she returned than Trevian was already knocking on their door.

Adriena answered the door, saying, "Gosh, that was mighty quick. I thought it would be at least an hour."

Trevian replied, "Normally it would be, but I was already on my way here."

"Will you be staying through lunch with us? I can ask Mr. Bonnaire and request it."

"Are you sure? It is my understanding your mother is to be here."

Serenity watched the two of them with a smile on her face, and then said, "Yes, Sister! Please do go and ask. I insist. You never know when I may need a doctor around."

A funny knowing look passed between the twin sisters, and they both broke into matching grins. Yes, there were definitely times that they looked like each other. It was in little things, smiles or winks or even just nuances when they spoke or moved. Adriena gave her sister that look as she responded, "Very well, I shall return in a moment."

While she was gone, Trevian thoroughly checked Serenity, making sure that she was just having morning sickness. He said, "Looks like everything seems to be fine, other than your morning sickness. That drink seems to be helping, and it is healthy for you."

"Thank you, Trevian. May I say something about my sister?"

After hesitating just a bit, he said, "Sure. What is it you need to tell me?"

"Only that if I am reading you right, I should hope that you really like my sister. I know for a fact she likes you."

"Why are you telling me this?"

"I just needed you to know before you ever question it, and I know the signs well."

Looking at her curiously, he replied, "I shall keep that in mind."

Gently grabbing his arm, she said, "Please don't let her know I told you this!"

"Not a word, I promise," he said as he smiled.

Adriena, walking back in and noticing the look on their faces, said, "Did I miss something?"

Clearing his throat to answer, he ventured to ask, changing the subject, "Did you get a reply? Your sister is fine, other than just a little morning sickness. That drink you gave her is very helpful."

In the back of her mind, Adriena couldn't help but wonder what he was not telling her. Then she replied to his question, saying, "Yes, he is setting another place." Turning to Serenity, she said, "Here, try some juice and a little fruit. Let's see if you can keep these down. I heard Mother may be here soon. Want to try?"

"Okay, Adriena, I will try to eat this."

Serenity ate what she could, and said, "I think I will be fine, and I am still hungry. When did you say lunch will be ready?"

The room filled with laughter after her remark. Markis came to see what was going on up there and said, "It looks as if you seem to be feeling much better, and the color is back in your cheeks. Just wanted you girls to know your mother is on her way so you can be ready when she arrives. Lunch will be ready within an hour."

"Yes, sir," they all responded, and Trevian walked with him to lend a hand for whatever was needed while the girls readied themselves for their mother's arrival.

"Adriena, after we talk with Mother today, I will be leaving. I should have the answers I seek on the morrow and leave at first light."

"Serenity, please stay here. You need to think about the baby!"

"Adriena, you know I must find a way to get my Darien back. There is an entrance to the cave that is not far from where the war is taking place. I know if we can get him there, we will be able to live out our lives, but it will be in hiding from Father. That is a chance I am willing to take, and I intend on doing it. No one, I mean no one, will change my mind on this! The only reason I tell you now is because I need your help. It will be very hard for me to do this on my own. Can I please count on you to help me?"

With complete thought of what was at stake, she understood her sister and said this in her plea: "Serenity, you know I will do anything for you. This is very dangerous, and you are carrying my only niece or nephew. If anything should ever happen to either of you, I will not forgive myself for letting you do this. Please, I beg of you to reconsider what you ask of me."

"Adriena, I know what I ask is hard to do, but I shudder to think what will happen to the one I love! I will not forgive myself if I know there is at least one way to help him. Yes, it would be easier were I not with child, but I will have a father to raise his child without any sight of war, if at all possible. Know I have thought this through, and I really believe this can work. Please, Adriena, do this for me. I promise to be very careful, and I'll take every precaution into consideration. Just know that with or without your help, I am going to give it all I've got and try. I wouldn't do this if I didn't believe with every fiber of my being that I could do this. I believe wholeheartedly this can work… Please, will you help me? I must do this!"

"Serenity, you know I will do this, on one condition."

"Name it. What do you ask, Adriena?"

"Trevian is to come with us. I will have the best care for my sister's needs, and I'll not take no for an answer. Will you agree to these terms?"

"Yes, Adriena, I will agree, but I can't help but wonder if my sister wants him to come for other reasons!" she said as she smiled.

"That may be so, Serenity, but I assure you, your needs will be before my own. Okay, it sounds like Mother has arrived. Are you ready to go down and see her?"

"Yes, let's go before my father-in-law sends someone to get us."

They linked arms as they walked out the door, laughing at the thought of what they'd just said.

Chapter 22

Unveiling past

Markis looked up to see them coming and heard their giggles of laughter. He said, "And just what is so funny?" Noticing their mother, Adriena looked at her sister and said, "Just an inside joke. Nothing important."

Arabel looked at her daughters and said, "Oh! How I have missed you girls. I do hope that one day we can be a family again. Until then, I have no choice except to take what I can get. I have much to tell you, and I will after we have lunch."

Markis looked at her then and said, "Let's see what we have on today's menu now, shall we?"

After the girls hugged their mother, they headed to the prepared table. They sat down to a wonderful meal of roasted leg of lamb that was every bit as good as the wafting aromas had promised.

Arabel spoke up and said, "Markis, I don't believe you've introduced me to this fine young man!"

"Oh! Where are my manners? Arabel, this is Trevian. He has just graduated and is a very fine doctor, trained by his father. He medically takes care of the girls while his father was called to aid in this stupid war."

"I see, and Serenity is taken care of with everything she has going on?"

Serenity spoke up. "Mom, everything is fine, and your grand baby is in good health. Isn't that right, Trevian?"

Feeling a little awkward in the conversation, Trevian said, "Yes, ma'am, they both are doing as well as can be expected."

Markis, noticing the uneasiness, said, "How about we finish our meal and talk about this later, okay?"

Arabel, noticing his expression, said, "Yes, of course. My compliments to your cooks for a very fine meal."

It was obvious that Trevian was feeling relieved when the conversation took a different turn. His gaze wandered to Adriena. Which wasn't lost on Arabel. Adriena smiled back, not really concerned over what her mother thought.

Adjourning to the family room, Arabel noticed the drink Adriena gave to Serenity. She said, "How long has your sickness been going on? I can't help but notice what you are drinking. I had the same thing with the nausea I had to endure."

Serenity said, "Oh, Mom, I've been so sick with this morning sickness, off and on since only a few days after I found out I was expecting. Yes, I have found that it really does help."

With a hint of a smile, Arabel said, "I'm glad to notice you girls paid attention to some of the things I did."

"Mom?" Serenity said, "I sure would appreciate if you could let us know where Darien is. Do you happen to know the exact location? Please tell me the truth."

Arabel said, "Serenity, of course I'll tell you, based on a promise that you will not act on this foolish notion to find him. Think about your baby. Traveling during these times is dangerous for you both. How would you feel if you lost your baby, Darien's baby? This child could be your only child from Darien if he were to die in this war. Or what if you need emergency assistance for an unexpected early delivery due to all the travel… This could cause you to die. Just think of what it would do to Darien should he live and have no mother for his unborn child. I see no good coming out of this if you pursue your desire to go into the wilds to find him. You know this to be a foolish thing to try, right?"

"Mom, you know how much I love him and what I would do to get him back. After the last letters I received, I need to find a way. I fear Father is no longer himself and he no longer cares at all about what happens to his men. And especially to Darien. If there is anything you can do to reach him, please tell me a way. I will not have my husband go mad, all because of this damn war. I will make no promises, nor will my conscience let me say 'forget it.' I'm sorry, but I need to find him and bring him home."

"Serenity, please think about it, make a rational decision. Adriena, please talk some sense into your sister!"

Adriena said, "Mom! I am sorry, but I will not go against her wishes, no matter how much I truly disagree. You know, I feel what my sister feels. I feel her pain of not knowing, I feel the pain in her heart when she thinks of her love in miserable conditions and potentially in danger of life and limb. Doing things slowly will not help us this time. Things need to be done quickly and we will not sit idly by just to miss the window we may have as our best chance. Mother, you should know us well enough on this. Not trying to be disrespectful, but really!"

Arabel looked at Serenity and said, "Fine, then I shall do what I must. You may read that letter I am to give Markis." She looked at Markis and said, "I wrote this letter last night, and I wish for you to read this after I leave. Will you do this for me?"

"Arabel, what is this about? What are you going to do? I don't like the way this is going!"

"Markis, I am sorry, but I must do this. Please read the letter after I leave. You will understand when you read it."

Serenity said one more thing to her mother. "Mom, please, should you see or hear from Father, do not say a word about this baby. I mean it, not one word until Darien is safely in my arms again. Promise me you will not!"

Arabel said to her daughter, "Serenity, I promise I will do my best not to say a word. If you intend to proceed in whatever you decide to do, and if you fail, you leave me no choice. Do you understand?"

"Yes, Mother. I shall hold you to your promise. Now I must get some rest. It is nightfall and I am feeling very tired. Know that I do love you, and I really know that you know why I chose this path. I would gladly do it again if I had been given a chance to do this over. Why? You know why."

Before Serenity finished what she was saying, Arabel replied, "Yes, I know my daughters well, and you truly love him. The same as I did one other, long ago. The only difference is you pursued your happiness, where I did not, and I am happy for you in this decision. I just want what's best in your life, so please don't shut me out."

Serenity hugged her mother, tears pooling in her eyes and slowly traveling down her cheeks as she said, "I love you too, Mother, and I want you to be a part of our lives. Just know that without Darien, this cannot be the way it should. Give me a reason that's good enough and I shall listen. That is all I can do."

As the girls left to go upstairs, Trevian turned to Markis and said, "I need to check on Serenity one more time before she retires." Secretly, Trevian thrilled at the thought of being with Adriena again and was delighted to have this excuse to leave with them. He walked with the girls, at Adriana's side, hopeful that they might have a few moments alone.

After he did a final checkup, the discussion centered on when to leave. Serenity said, "I have enough provisions and have everything packed for the journey. Darien had me learn the ways of these caves, so I know a way to find him by winding through the tunnels, using them to stay out of sight. I know this sounds foolhardy, but I believe it is the best chance we've got. Adriena, you know I cannot stay here.

I have to try, and without me, you'll never find your way through these caves."

Adriena turned to Trevian and said, "Trevian, thank you for coming to check on Serenity."

He replied, "If I may, would you walk with me on the way out? I would like to talk with you for a little bit." They left the room and got to the landing, where he said, "I know you don't like the idea of Serenity leaving to find Darien, but she is strong and in good health. Unless she does something really stupid, she should be fine. We can take things slowly. I think the trail through these mountains is shorter than if we had to go the normal way…and we won't have to worry about being seen on the roads and hiding."

"Thank you for the comforting words, Trevian. It makes me feel better, but I still want to try and talk Serenity out of going." With that, Adriena turned back toward the bedroom door.

Softly brushing Serenity's hair out of her eyes, Adriena said, "Is there nothing we can say to change your mind? Darien would be furious to know you are taking such an enormous risk. He would expect me to keep you from doing this."

"Adriena, you understand my reason, and I'll not have him turn out like our father. Mother knows this pain, and I will do everything I can to not let this go any further."

All Adriena could say, while wiping the tears from her eyes, was "Let's get some rest before tomorrow comes. It will be too soon."

Adriana did nothing but shake her head in agreement to Serenity, and then turned the lights out to sleep. How hard sleep came this night... So much to think about and to ruminate on in her head! The feelings for Trevian that caused her heart to flutter and what seemed to be ticklish butterflies to come alive within her whenever he was near. Even now as she thought of him and remembered his musky scent, the way he so confidently carried his body with a lithe stride and a tender touch as he surveyed Serenity's condition.

She rolled over to her other side, thinking perhaps this way the stress that had built up in her neck would dissipate and she would find sleep. But that wasn't to be. Not at this moment. Her mother came to mind now, and all the feelings she had tucked away since this whole business with Serenity and Darien had come up. As she relaxed, she remembered all the times she had yearned to just be "one" with her mother. But she and Serenity were always two. There was rarely "alone" time with her mother. Yet she and Serenity were so tightly connected that their feelings toward each other and their understanding of each other was a bond normally reserved for mother and child. At this moment, Adriena wished she also had that connection with her mother. The last few moments before sleep claimed Adriena were filled with memories of her mother's loving touches, embraces, and hugs. Yes, she would love to be closer to her mother and hoped it would be possible to move forward with this plan after their current plans were realized. If only…

Arabel said, "Markis, I'm just going to tell you what is in the letter. I fear my Tomáš has changed for the worst. I can bear this pain no longer. If it is as bad as I've been told, then I no longer have a choice. I must go and find a way to convince him he is wrong. I take full responsibility for my actions and I will accept whatever my fate is to be. Please tell my girls that I love them and will do everything I can to help them."

"Arabel! Don't do this. I beg you, please! Let us find another way together. There has to be one!"

She raised her hand quickly, silencing his words by laying her fingers across his lips, saying, "Markis, you know full well I am the only one that has any chance possible to reach him. It will be a difficult journey, but I must do this."

"Arabel, I insist you take some of my men to see you safely there, and I will not take no for an answer!"

"Very well, I will agree to this. And Markis?" she said as she looked at him. "Thank you for everything you've done, especially for my girls. I am glad it was you they turned to when they wouldn't listen to me. I have no idea how we are to repay you."

"Arabel, there is no need. Besides, we are now family, with our first grandchild on the way."

As they both smiled at the thought, she said, "Thank you. I mean it. Now, I shall take my leave at first light, and will return home."

Chapter 23

Storms Coming

Next morning, Serenity, in a quickened pace, hurried to the restroom without any warning. Adriena, startled, woke up to check on her. She ran quietly to the kitchen to fix Serenity something to ease her symptoms, and hoped to make this journey easier. As she returned to the room, Serenity emerged from the bathroom.

"Serenity, here drink this." After handing her the drink and watching her a few minutes, she said, "Serenity, I worry, and I do love you, dear sister. Although I understand your reason, I still wish you would reconsider this foolishness."

"Adriena, I need to do this. I've read some of the letters Mom and Dad wrote to each other. I will not let Darien suffer this same fate. From everything I've seen and witnessed, I will find a way to help him before the madness takes over. Tell me, have you read the letters?"

"Honestly, Serenity, I can't say that I have. I know there is no changing your mind, but know I will protect you at all costs, and I'll do what must be done. You have my promise on that, okay?"

"Adriena, I believe in your promise, and I thank you for believing in me. Love you, Sis!"

Adriena hugged her sister and said, "I love you too, Serenity. Now, we need to get going if we are to make good time. Are you feeling well enough to travel now?"

Serenity nodded her head and replied, "Yes, I'm ready. Let's go."

They met up with Trevian at the small opening and headed to the caves on the way to Serenity's beloved Darien. Adriena was so grateful that Trevian had procured a small donkey on which they loaded their meager supplies. They were traveling light, to move more quickly.

The day had dawned beautifully, but Darien did not see any of the beauty. He was taken out for more punishment. The whippings were harsh, and often included kicks in the ribs or punches in the face. Just enough to keep him painfully alive. Now he had deep purple bruises over yellow bruises and black bruises. There were cuts all over his back. Some were deep and needing attention. He clung to life, thinking of the loved one he left behind. In his mind, he called for Serenity as the weather changed and thunderheads formed in the near distance. A storm was brewing, and lightning cracked. The air changed. A coldness entered his chamber and a dampness was creeping into what had been his clothes, but were now just shreds being held next to his skin by the blood from his oozing cuts. Darien felt the need to gather what strength was left in him. He knew he would need this to find his way back to her as soon as he could. As he faded in and out of consciousness, he held Serenity's beautiful image within his vision, remembering the warmth of her embrace, and the last long nights together in the caves when he'd showed her all the twists and turns of the tunnels. They had made it a game of hide-and-seek at times. He didn't want her to worry about getting lost if she ever needed to use this as an escape route. Sometimes he gave her a light that went out while he was hidden… He would call and she would find him. Always getting more familiar with the tunnels. It was a fun game and as new lovers they always had a reward at reunion. Yes, he would linger on those happy thoughts, and they carried him through the darkest times. Then his thoughts turned to their unborn child. Would it be a boy or a girl? Sometimes in his delirious moments, he envisioned a daughter that was a miniature image of his mother. He had to live. He could not die. He needed to get back to Serenity and their unborn child. Oh, the longing so deep inside him always brought back strength.

He said aloud, "Serenity, I promise, I will find my way back to you. There has to be a way!" Exhaustion finally claimed his mind and body. As he drifted off to sleep, he sent Serenity his dreams, hoping that they could connect through dreams as she dreamed too.

The time went quickly as they traveled along a rocky path, making their way as fast as possible. Knowing it could take a few days to get to Darien, they stopped and rested as much as was necessary, given Serenity's condition. Nightfall was near, which was nearly unnoticed within the cave's continuous twilight, but now with the rumble in their tummies, it was apparent that a longer stop for dinner and the night was required. It was still a sparse meal––a slice of bread with dried meat. But this time, since they were now at a break in the cave, they were in a small open area where a small waterfall tumbled over a cliff's edge. On the creek bed there was natural lettuce sometimes known as miner's lettuce that added some nice moisture to the otherwise dry sandwich. A little further off was some dry brush to use for a small fire. How nice to have a hot cup of tea and rest their weary feet.

Serenity looked at her sister and said, "Adriena, I'm feeling helpless to surrender, forced beyond my control. Through a silent prayer of his heart, I can hear him calling my name as the winds howl and the lightning cracks overhead." Tears began to flow down Serenity's cheeks, and Adriena pulled her sister close in a warm embrace to comfort her.

Adriena said, "I promise you, we are going to do everything we can to get him back."

Markis rode out to see his son and tend to his wounds. The thunderstorms were rolling overhead as he galloped down the road toward the camp. At least, he was hoping that it was only thunder and not military arms! But soon the reflections of lightning brightened the horizon and the streaking tongues of white light darted overhead. Like white-hot whips, lightning now bolted closely, making the hair on his arms stand up straight as the tip of the whip lashed into a tree close by. What an onslaught! What war was going on in the heavens? Who were the battle participants? Markis rode like the wind, praying as he went for protection from the earthshaking peals that elevated the sharp gallop of his horse into a breathtaking run. Yes, it was also his favorite stallion that sensed the danger they were in, riding through this horrible storm. The sheets of rain falling made it feel as if they were riding through an unending waterfall. Where was all this water coming from? And where would it go? Oh, he had seen the mountain gullies fill ever so quickly, and even the tunnels in the mountain were not immune to the rushing water needing to find lower grounds, and then eventually the lakes and oceans.

What of Serenity and Adriena, were they safe? They would be on their way through the tunnels of the mountains. Had Darien, in the short time he had to show Serenity the secret passageway, remembered that there could be danger in the passages? The storm was moving on. The rain continued, but the thunderous rumbles and the lightning whips drew farther and farther to the west. Markis drew up a bit on the reins and felt his prized steed slow a bit from the breakneck speed to a slower gallop. Even the muscles in the horse's body began to relax as he realized that the imminent danger had passed. Totally drenched, the pair arrived at the military camp and came to an abrupt stop in front of the detention cave. Given the war footing, it was unusual that Markis could just ride in like that without being questioned. Perhaps it was the storm, but still this would not have happened under his command. He made a mental note.

A salute from the guard and a quick nod, and then he was inside the irregular cave opening. As his eyes adjusted to the dim light filtering in from the small barred hole serving as a window, he saw that Darien was passed out on a cot. Thank God, at least he had a cot and mustn't sleep on the cold, hard, and disgustingly dirty floor. As Markis moved closer to his sleeping son, the stench of rat pee filled his nose and the rat feces underfoot ground into dust. He listened closely while advancing into the cold, stark cell, hoping his son would wake to speak. But Darien was in a deep, deep sleep, where pain was absent and dreams forever ran in the mind. With visions of Serenity, he began talking in his sleep.

"Serenity, my love, not a moment goes by that I don't long to see you. I long to hold you in my arms again. Just to caress the worries from your mind. I long to see your electrifying blue eyes that penetrate the very depths of my soul. I fight for you and I'll hang on until the day you're in my arms again. I long to see your face and to feel the peace you hold within. You give me hope, and light my path to quell the rage I hold within. Forgive me, my love, as I fight for my very existence. Dwindle the flames within, oh, please let peace overwhelm the heat of these flames. It only takes a few words from you. You whom I hold so dear. I love you and I will fight to hang on with every ounce of strength to life just to see you once again." Then he drifted off with no more words as his father wrote the words spoken so that Serenity would know everything he said. He tended to Darien's wounds, bathing the festering cuts and putting cold compresses on the bruises, in hopes of making him well again. Then he left the dark, cold cave and went to the camp to see the man who used to be a close friend. He told the officer at the entrance of the tent that he must speak to Tomáš.

"I'm sorry, sir, he says he is busy and to come back at a later time."

"I'm sorry to do this, soldier, but my rank supersedes yours and I will talk with him now." With a determined scowl, Markis walked past him and stood in front of Tomáš and said, "Tomáš, this has got to stop! Now, my friend—or at least you were once my friend. What has happened to you? Where is the friend I once had long ago? Surely he is still there?"

"I'm sorry, Markis, but this is war, and I must attend to my duties. You know I hold this cause in the highest regard, and I must not sacrifice this cause for anything or anyone!"

"You're telling me you would sacrifice your own family for a cause that can be dealt with another way for the sake of peace?"

"My family is not here and I'll do anything to keep them safe."

"Tomáš! You are wrong, my friend. Your wife comes to plead one last time for you. Oh, and just so you know, you will not harm my son any longer. I should have a father for my grandchild."

"My apologies, Markis, but he is paying the price for his transgressions in disobeying my direct orders!" he said as he turned his back upon his friend, knowing that what he had just said was wrong.

"Tomáš! You are not hearing me. Open your heart, man! That grandchild I speak of is the same as yours."

"Markis, that cannot be, I forbade either of my daughters to have anything to do with him."

"Yes, Tomáš, that was loud and clear. I should like to tell you. Serenity and my son married in secret in a bond that cannot be broken. He is your son-in-law and they do have a child on the way. Tomáš, I beg you to let him go to her. They have a love that is very rare to see. Would you begrudge the happiness they seek? Or would you destroy everything held dear--all for the sake of this damn war!

Isn't this war to save our families? Why would you then want to destroy what you seek to save?"

"Wait a minute, my daughter did what! Married! No, this cannot be! I forbade it! They knew full well not to cross that path!" Tomáš angrily paced in deep thought and then said, "If what you say is true, hear me, old friend, that changes nothing!"

"So, friend! You would do this to Arabel, who loves you with all her heart. You would take away the one piece of happiness that could change the entire family? I knew you once to be reasonable, but this, my friend, is unforgivable, and it will be you that has to live with these consequences. Know this, I will pull rank if I need to, and you will not harm my son any further. You know my rank is much higher. You will release my son and turn from this path you're on, my friend!"

"Markis, I serve the commander over this platoon and I am strictly following his orders. Unless your rank is above his, I have no choice. I suggest you leave and do not come back unless you have the correct documents to change the way this is going. Only then can you overturn my command. You are my friend and I will allow you the time needed to accomplish what is needed. As for your son, I cannot release him."

Tomáš asked his men to leave. "I should like to talk with my friend alone." He waited for them to leave and then continued.

"Old friend, you know I would let your son go if it were only up to me. The only way he could ever leave is if he could escape. He would have to stay in hiding until after the war." As he leaned forward with a look of a madman he said, "Know that if he returned, his punishment would be much more severe. All I can say is he needs a place well hidden, do you understand? I only tell you this because you are my oldest and dearest friend. You know what the last war did to me. I don't know how much more I can withstand. If you know of a way that can turn this war to the good, please tell me. I'm all ears. You must show documented proof, do you understand?"

"Yes, I do, old friend. I promise you, I will do everything in my power to change this. Please, Tomáš, I beg of you to permit me or my physician's son to take care of my son while he is here."

"Markis, you have my leniency on this matter and that is all I can do. Nothing else, understand? Oh, and one more thing: if anything should happen to me, please take care of my Arabel. I could not bear the thought of her with anyone else. I know she loved you once, and I believe you can help her through anything should that time ever arise. Give my grandchild my love and all that he or she deserves. I am under surveillance; that is why I tell you while no one is here, and this may be the only chance I can say this. So please, forgive me, my friend."

"Tomáš, I wish for you to tell them yourself. They need to hear this from you. Promise me you will at least try. You are a warrior. I wish for you to keep that honor alive and well, my friend."

"Markis, I do not know what our future holds and this is the last time I will speak of this. I tell you these things because you are my friend and always will be. Take this letter and hide it well. Do not read it unless something happens to me, understand? Our time has expired and I must return to my duties. I fear there is a spy in the mix and I must carry out what was started."

"Tomáš, you must hear one more thing. I believe Arabel is on her way to see you. Know, my friend, I tried to stop her."

"No! It cannot be. She will be in the highest danger! Markis, you must take her home. Keep her as safe as possible."

"As you wish. I will do what I can. If I may inquire she stay in my home. You know I have the safest in all the lands. That is the only reason I ask. We both seek what is in her best interest, do we not?"

155

Tomáš thought a minute or so and replied, "I will consider it only for that reason. I owe you much. A debt that I'm afraid will be hard to pay. Now go, tend to your son while I attend to my duties."

Tomáš laid a gentle hand on his shoulder with a little compassion. Then he walked out and said to the guard, "Soldier, see that he tends to his son. He is granted a pardon only because he is a physician and a ranking officer."

"Yes, sir! Right away!" Then he escorted Markis, as requested.

Chapter 24

Unexpected

Serenity, Adriena, and Trevian made their way to the opening just ahead, as they went down a different path shown by Darien to Serenity before he left and they stopped before exiting to rest a bit. This last day had been tough. They had left early in the morning, awoken by the sound of rushing waters. The small stream, which had cascaded so nicely over the cliff, had become a menacing waterfall. It was a stroke of luck that they had moved their campsite to the far side of the clearing and into the cavern when the thunderstorm had sent the first drops of pelleting rain. They had gathered their meager belongings and were able to keep them dry on the higher-lying path within the cavern. Morning came too soon, because the night was too short. The thunder and lightning rumbled and cracked for longer than they would have liked. But eventually exhaustion took over. Now they had covered several miles with Serenity riding the donkey. The little beast carried Serenity easily and even some of their provisions. However, Trevian made a pack from his cloak and strapped the food supplies and his doctor's medical pack on his back.

The sun was bright after the continuous dimness of the cavern and they squinted as they found a mossy patch not too soggy to take a quick break.

Adriena looked at her sister questioningly. She started to open her mouth to say something. Halting her, Serenity said, "I'm fine. I can do this."

Adriena said, "Who are you trying to convince? Me or yourself? Serenity, you look as if you're running a fever. Please, let Trevian do a quick exam. This is going to be the hardest part to go through, and you need to be one hundred percent. I need you to stay well. Now! Let him do what needs to be done, okay?"

Serenity nodded her head in response. She hadn't been feeling well for some time now and had welcomed the opportunity to ride, even though it meant that her sister and Trevian had to carry items as they walked. She felt guilty, but even so, she felt rather weak, and very, very warm, even after exiting the cool cavern.

Trevian looked, took a quick survey of his patient, and said, "You're not going to like what I say, but please, just hear me out." Serenity, with a saddened face, lowered her head as she nodded in response. She had been trying so very hard to pull herself together. Willing her body to be strong. She needed to be strong. She had to get to Darien.

Trevian continued, "You know, this is hard for me to say, but not all of this is bad, okay?" While shaking her head at the same time, she listened to what he said. "Serenity, this journey has been taxing on your body and you know it isn't good for you or the baby. Even riding has been taking strength from you. Therefore, you need to rest, and I mean for a day or so. That's the bad news. The good news is, I have something I can give you, a natural remedy. I believe it will help you, but it will take anywhere from a couple of days to a week. You need to rest before we go anywhere else."

Serenity started to open her mouth to say something to protest, but before she could, Trevian shook his head to keep her silent.

He continued, "I'm sorry, Serenity, but you must rest before we go. Doctor's orders. If it will ease your mind, I will go check on him, and I will see if anything has changed. While I'm there, I will see what the easiest access is. Under no circumstance is your father to see you, is that understood?"

With a heavy heart, Serenity and Adriena replied with, "Yes, we understand." Serenity added, "But I don't like it at all."

Trevian said, "Adriena, I need to speak with you before I go. May I?" and pointed into the direction of a secluded area. Holding his hand out like a gentleman would, he said, "Serenity, I hope you don't mind."

Serenity looked up with a big smile toward Adriena and said, "No, not at all." She was happy for her sister, yet saddened because of this damn war. The soft tufts of moss on the mound welcomed her growing frame and she leaned back against a sandy embankment with a sigh. How could she go on? How lucky she felt that Trevian had come with them. She was so focused on Darien, she had nearly forgotten the child she carried. No, she would listen and rest. She did not want any harm to come to this special child. The reminder and symbol of the pure love between her and Darien. This was all she would have of him if the unthinkable happened in this stupid war. As she continued to relax, exhaustion crept into every bone and settled in. As exhaustion called took over her body, slumber encased her troubled mind. Mercifully, the light breeze started to cool her feverish body, bringing the scent of wildflowers into the dreams forming in her tortured mind. In minutes, Serenity was sound asleep. Always the attentive sister, Adriena made sure she was comfortable, then walked to Trevian.

As soon as they were alone, he swiftly pulled her close, locking his hands behind her back. His eyes focused on Adriena's lithe form, her tangled hair, which straggled down her forehead. Always looking after Serenity, and with such love and compassion. He had never met someone who showed such tenderness and was so selfless. Yes, Adriena was beautiful. He had been immediately attracted to her.

But it was her being. The person who was so selfless and humble, yet spirited, that he had fallen in love with. "Make no mistake," Trevian had said to himself, "this girl is made of steel. Don't let her soft outward beauty fool you." Only a few inches away, he took his fingers and lightly caressed her lips. He held her gaze only for a moment before he deeply and affectionately kissed her.

Losing all her senses, Adriena forgot why she was there. This moment was theirs alone… He removed some of her clothing from her shoulders, one piece at a time, softly caressing his lips across them. He proceeded to keep her captivated, removing more, one by one. She stopped him briefly with her elevated breathing before he removed the last to say in a whisper, "What about my sister? What if she wakes?"

Holding her gaze intently, not letting her utter another word, he said, "Did you really get a good look at her? She is exhausted. I wouldn't be surprised if she slept for hours. Besides, she knows how we feel. And I don't really think she would mind me having a few moments alone with you. I love you and I want you here and now. I don't want to lose any chance on the what-ifs—that is, if you feel the same as I do?"

"Of course, I love you and Serenity knows well how I feel. I just never thought…" She paused, holding his gaze, and said, "Oh, the hell with what I thought," and kissed him back willingly.

He broke for a moment and whispered breathlessly, "Are you absolutely sure?"

She pulled him close to urge him on, not uttering a word only a nod of her head yes.

He laid her back slowly taking her shirt off as he kissed her lips, with a light caress moving toward the bareness of her shoulder down to just above her breast. He moves further down arousing her senses sending a sensation releasing in a breathless moan escaping her lips. Trevian slides the rest of what she was wearing off, just below her

160

naval moving his hand between her thighs penetrating deeply as her body moved to every thrust. Adriena closed her eyes taking in the moment as he slid inside harder and faster.

Her breathing whispering heavier in his ear making her yearn for more. In her mind she says his name over and over again, letting the moans escape echoing through the entrance of the cave. He holds her hands in place as he moves deeper with the bareness of the skin lightly grazing hers, igniting an electrified explosion welling inside reaching that pivotal climax in heated bliss. A passion they share down to the final ecstasy giving in to their love and desire.

At last, she opened her eyes as he rolled off onto the soft moss-covered ground in the shade of a beautiful lilac bush. Unknowingly, they had retreated into a shaded mossy landing near the side of the mountain. Vines hung from lichen-covered trees, and lush wild lilac bushes had served up fragrance from their blue flowers as they unintentionally bumped into them. This first time of their lovers' tryst could not have had a more perfect place. No warm bed or sunny couch would have equaled the beauty of this natural enclave. Yes, it was natural for them to be together. Adriena knew that he was her beloved. She looked over at him, taking him in… His lean torso, the hardened muscles, strong arms and legs. Ohhhh.

He turned, holding her in his arms' embrace, and saw the intense gaze in her eyes. It was as if this look were electrifying her very soul, and he said, "You are so beautiful, it is as if the sun were illuminated in your face. You are absolutely radiant. I wish to never leave your side. I'd marry you with your consent."

"Is that what you call a proposal?" She smiled as she said it.

"No." He kneeled before her as he took her hand and said, "I loved you from the time I first saw your face." He reached over and fumbled in his trousers to pull a ring from his pocket and continued, "This belonged to my mother. I know we haven't been together long. You excite my very soul with a passion I never want to lose. I love you more every day I see you." Looking deeply within her eyes, he said, "Adriena, would you do me the honor of becoming my wife?"

Completely blown away by his mere presence, before she realized it, she heard her voice saying, "Yes, I will marry you. I feel the same as you."

With a smile, he slipped the ring on her finger, surprisingly the right size, and kissed her once again, melting her inner strength.

Now, gathering her senses, she stopped to say, "We need to check on my sister. I worry so much about her."

They quickly got dressed, their gazes never wavering from each other as they walked back hand in hand.

Serenity was now awake and watching them walk back to her. Raising an eyebrow, she looked at her sister and said, "Just where have you two have been? I was about to come find you, and just what have you been doing all this time?" Looking at their wrinkled clothes and hair in a mess, she said, "Never mind, I have a good idea."

Adriena said coyly, "And just what is it you think you know?"

"It doesn't take a genius to know. You forget I've been there."

Playing innocent, Adriena said, "Oh? And where is it you think I've been?"

Looking at them both smiling, she said, "For starters, your clothes are wrinkled more than they were."

"Serenity, it's been a long walk. Besides, we've slept in them a few times. That should be understandable."

Serenity loved making her sister squirm every chance she could. "Okay, then I'd love to hear the explanation about your hair. I believe that is a dead giveaway."

Trevian started laughing as Adriena said, "There's nothing wrong with my hair!"

He laughed harder, then pulled grass and twigs from it.

Serenity looked dead at her sister and said, "There hasn't been any grass for miles." There was no holding back as laughter filled the air, and then Serenity sat back down.

Trevian said to Serenity, "Your sister has something to tell you, and I am getting my things together. There is much to discuss while I get ready to see Darien. I will be back as soon as I am able. While I'm there, I will survey the land to see how we are to proceed. I overheard that your mother would be here and my father was to come with Markis."

Adriena looked at her sister and said, "If our mother is to be here, we need to be extremely cautious while we are here. Serenity, that is why we need you at a hundred percent, okay?"

"I understand, Adriena, I will do what I must."

Trevian said, "There is one more thing we will need to do. We may need to move quickly should that time come and must be prepared for anything. Whatever happens, we must make it back here safely, no matter what or…" He trailed off to shutter the thought, just shaking his head. Then he looked up and said, "We will make it back, right?"

Both young ladies said yes in agreement. Serenity looked into the distance and thought about what life without a father would be like for this child. She remembered how difficult it had been when her father was off to the last war, and she was at least lucky enough to have known him. No, her child would have a father. She would do anything to be sure that Darien got back safely. Serenity said to herself, just above a whisper but loud enough for them to hear her words, "I will have a father for this baby!"

Trevian finished packing the few things he needed, leaving the food, blankets, and all the cooking utensils, and said to Adriena, "I must go and find him before dark. Please promise me you both will wait here for my return. I will not be gone for maybe a day or two before I come back to see if you are able to travel the distance."

Looking dead at Adriena, he said, "Damn, you're so beautiful! I don't want to stay away from you too long." Then he embraced her into a kiss, with Serenity not missing a beat between them.

Breaking from their embrace, Adriena said, as she ran her finger down his mouth and poked him affectionately in the chest, "You had better hurry back as soon as you can!" After kissing her one last time, Trevian reluctantly jogged off into the forest.

Serenity looked into her sister's flushed face and said in a dead-serious tone, "Okay! Spill it. The obvious look on your face says you love him. So what is it he wishes for you to tell me?"

"I can see, Serenity, you don't miss much at all, do you?"

"Not if it is the same as I feel for Darien."

While shaking her head, Adriena said, "I suppose it is the same." Then she showed the ring to her.

Excited for her sister, perhaps a little shocked at the timing, she said, "When? Must have been that roll in the hay while I was sleeping, wasn't it?"

"Yes it was, and he asked just before we came back to you."

While smiling, Serenity said, "And what was your answer, as if I don't already know?" Knowing full well she could read it in her eyes and the smile was a dead giveaway.

Serenity squeezed her sister and said, "I'm so happy for you guys," then sat down into deep thoughts of her own.

Adriena, reading her like a book, said, "Don't worry, Serenity, I promise we will get him back." Then she sat beside her, laying Serenity's head on her shoulder in comfort while tears trickled down her cheeks.

Chapter 25

Field of Escape

Trevian walked the trails carefully. He watched from all angles with great caution until he could reach the safest area. It was a half a day's walk to the caves where Darien was being held, so he made every minute of the day count. In the distance he could hear gunfire, which never dissipated. The night sky was red overhead and heralded a storm in the distance. He made his way through the last part of the trails. Just as he reached the caves, a soldier said, "STOP."

Markis just happened to be near and said, "It's okay, Private, he may enter. Let him pass, he is with me."

The private, with a questionable look on his face, replied, "Very well, just show me who you are. I just need your documented proof and then you can enter."

After examining the identification, the private said, "You may proceed, Dr. Trevian Strombalini."

After passing the guard, Trevian looked at Markis and said, "What was that all about?"

"Tomáš thinks it's necessary to post a guard as protection for us, when truly he is trying to control who comes in and out of here. Now what brings you here, son?"

"Sir, I need to speak to you with no ears overhearing our conversation."

"Very well, follow me." Markis took him into the cave and down the cavern past the holding cell and into a small antechamber that was quite secluded, with no sound penetrating the walls. "Okay, son, go ahead, I should very much like to hear what you have to say. Then we shall go and see Darien. Before we do, I should warn you that I have given all I can give him for pain."

Trevian, not liking the sound of what he'd just heard, proceeded, saying, "Sir, have you found a way to get him out of here?"

"Trevian, there is one way I believe will work. Though I do not know the way he should travel. It is very dangerous here now." With a curious look on his face he said, "Why do you ask?"

"Sir, you know how stubborn those girls are!"

Markis cut him off, breaking in with these words: "Oh please, dear Lord, tell me––they did not come!"

With his head hung down, Trevian said, "I'm sorry, sir, but they would not listen, and you know Serenity is adamant to see him. That's the bad news. Here is the somewhat good news." In a whisper, he said, "I left them in some hidden caves not too far from here. The same that leads to your place."

"Damn it, I made it abundantly clear for them to stay put. Serenity sent a letter to her mother that I was able to see before it was sent." After he paused on the thought of Trevian's last words he said, "Wait a minute! You said not far from here?" A light bulb went off as Trevian nodded his head yes. Markis said, "Yes, this just might work."

"What will work, sir, if I might ask? Serenity needs to see him, before he is moved. Is there any way to make this happen?"

"No, Trevian, this is out of the question. Under no circumstance is she to come here!"

"Sir, I'm afraid it is too late for that. Besides, it may be enough to help him."

"Do you know how foolish this is?"

"Sir, I understand full well and we will use great caution. Besides, it is going to take more than just you and I to move him if at all at a faster pace. We will have greater odds with more help and would give him a fighting chance."

Markis, deep in thought, began to say, "I still think this to be foolish, but I agree we should use all resources that are available. Only now we have two to worry about instead of one. Let me have a day to think on this and see what I can come up with. I need to check on a few things before I consider this kind of danger, especially to my unborn grandchild."

"Sir, if it makes you feel any better, I don't like it the same as you. I, too, have much to lose."

"Oh, and how's that?"

"Adriena has won my heart, and I have asked her to marry me."

"Trevian! Are you mad, in this day and time!" He shook his head in disappointment, and then thought of his own son. He said, "No, I suppose you're not, and I believe I can understand it. I'm sure this will be an interesting conversation you will have with your own father."

"I suppose. Though he does not know I've asked her, he does know of my feelings."

"Son, for your sake, I hope he opens up with open arms to welcome her." They laughed together. Then Markis said, "Come on! Let's check on my son." With a smile they walked toward his holding cell. Then Trevian's smile faded from his face.

"Sir, what the hell have they done to him? He was not like this when I saw him last!"

"I'm sorry to tell you, but he has endured more punishment, and I'm afraid he cannot withstand any more. Which is why I want to remove him from here as soon as we can. I need you to take a look at him and see if he can travel. I am worried that he may not be able to."

Trevian took out his medical supplies to do a thorough check. After about an hour, he gave Darien some natural herbs. One was given to help withstand the pain and one was to help with his injuries. He looked up at Markis and said, "We need to give him this for a few days. If there are any changes, we should know at the earliest by noon tomorrow. I will then return to bring the girls here, and I will warn them ahead of time."

"Trevian, I know this may put more ill thoughts in her mind about her father. Know he fights with the warrior within him, and this is poisoning him from the inside. Wars of the past have surfaced and there is no easy way for him to overcome them. I need to find a way to help them understand this. Their mother will be arriving soon. My hope is that she can find a way to get through to him before it is too late. My fear is that it is already too late, yet we hope he still has a fighting chance."

"Sir, I will talk to Adriena first. I'll see if I can convince her to see the truth. Then, together, maybe we can talk to Serenity and help her see the truth. You know how difficult she can be. I will try."

"Son, you are right about her stubbornness. She is so much like her mother, and my son has much to learn. How about we get some rest for the night. There is plenty of room, so you can stay here tonight. Let's worry about the rest tomorrow."

"Yes, and I will show you the passage I speak of that is not far from here," replied Trevian.

As they settled in for the night, Trevian's mind held the image of his love. He didn't notice how hard the stone floor of the cave was under the wool blanket he had wrapped around his body. His quest was to save at least one life from the hands of a barbaric cause. Together his father and Markis would work side by side in hopes to extinguish this conflict. As he drifted off to sleep, he called to her in his mind, "Adriena."

As the day wore on and the sun climbed higher into the sky, it became evident that the heat was not doing Serenity any good. While the still-exhausted Serenity slept, Adriena moved their items to the grassy spot of her "tryst" with Trevian. It was a naturally protected enclave. The wild lilac stood guard all around, filtering both sun and wind, with the screening protecting them from any potential passersby. Adriena sliced some more bread and made a very small fire to boil water and brew herbal tea, then coaxed Serenity from her mossy cushions into the shaded grassy area. There wasn't much conversation, each sister drawn into their own dreams and worries for tomorrow. As the evening shadows lengthened and mealtime again approached, Adriena saw Serenity stirring. "You're looking much better, Serenity. The beads of sweat are gone from your brow and I can see a little more natural color in your face. Do you feel better?"

"Yes," replied Serenity. "My dear, dear sister, you have been so kind and such a help to me. The rest and the tea have refreshed my being. I am still tired, but not as exhausted as I was earlier today. I do believe that my fever is also gone."

"I'm so happy to hear you confirm what I have been observing, Serenity. Now let's share this apple and some more bread before we turn in for the night."

"Seriously, sister, I don't know if I can sleep anymore. I have slept most of the day, and now my mind just wanders aimlessly, seeking Darien. Running what-if scenarios, which have ambiguous endings. Please tell me again that all will be well. I need your encouragement. Please tell me that I haven't been foolish in my quest to find Darien."

"Serenity, we are in a good spot, and Trevian has gone ahead to reconnoiter Darien's position and evaluate the best course of action to follow tomorrow. Let's rest knowing that all the best will happen tomorrow. We can count on him to figure it out."

As a light breeze rustled through the sheltered area, the girls pulled up the blankets and snuggled a bit closer together, confident that tomorrow would bring good news and a plan. Adriena's last thoughts were on Trevian, as she remembered the touches and the sweet kisses that had been exchanged on this spot earlier today. She longingly rolled the ring Trevian had placed on her finger with the promise of his undying love and marriage proposal.

The next day, Trevian was up before dawn, checking on Darien. He needed to light the lanterns for better lighting. The wounds had stopped their festering and the inflamed areas were now cool to the touch. Darien, still asleep, did not rouse during Trevian's tender inspections. Only moments later, Markis checked in and conferred with Trevian. "How is he doing?"

"Sir, he is doing a lot better. The herbal poultices have pulled the feverish infection from his worst wounds, and it also appears that the infection is diminishing. The tonic I gave him also seems to be helping. I was hoping he would respond quickly. It looks like he has."

"Can he be moved tomorrow?"

"Should be no problems with that, as long as he continues in this improvement. I will have no reason to object to his being moved."

"Trevian? I need you to do exactly what I say. I am sending you with a few of my men to help you to safely vacate this area and go back to update the girls. They will wait for you and escort you back here safely with them. They will not go all the way with you, since they have no need to know where the hidden and secret trails are. In fact, it is better that they do not know. Be careful in your return that no one follows you. Hide your tracks. It will take a bit longer, but use a circuitous route, and when returning with the sisters, do the same. Do not use the same route each time. We don't need to have a worn path to be followed by searchers. Never thought I would be happy that our forces don't use dogs." He sighed. "But I surely am now. It will work all the better for us. I don't want anything going wrong or to take any more chances than necessary. My men will bring you to this secret entrance to this detention cavern, so no one will be aware. I need you to hurry, please hurry. I want my son away from here as quickly as we can get him away. Alaster, Joffery, and Tallon will escort you, and they know the way you need to go without being noticed. Now go while you have a window."

"Yes, sir, I will hurry and quickly return, taking care to not leave easily followed trails."

Trevian met up with the trio and Alaster greeted him with a nod, saying, "Let's go this way, down through this narrow crevice. It looks like it goes nowhere, but if we squeeze through the left fissure, the way opens a bit, and we can move quickly another three hundred feet before coming to an equally narrow and well-hidden opening to the forest."

Alaster was right. After they moved carefully through the dark cavern with only the dim light from the left fissure, the tunnel widened. Squeezing through wasn't easy, and Trevian wondered how in the world they could get Darien through if he had to be supported. Well, not to worry about that now. Somehow it would be accomplished. The light of the early morning sun was dazzling upon climbing out to the cave. Yes, it was well hidden, and the foursome was careful not to disturb the brush concealing the entrance, and thankful that there was soft moss covering the ground. Trevian was grateful for the moss, thinking as he stepped onto the soft surface just behind the shrubbery, as opposed to grass, did not leave the telltale tracks of flattened grass for nosy followers or diligent searchers. Only a few more minutes and they reached the predetermined boundary line.

"We'll wait for you here and watch for your return with the girls."

Not wasting any time, Trevian hurried off to the south and melted into a stand of fir trees, using the pine needles covering the ground to hide his tracks. Then he turned east to the cave entrance.

He waited a few minutes to catch his breath, and looked around. Where were the girls? There was no sign of them. He thought surely they would have stayed directly there at the entrance where they had previously camped. A cold sweat started on his neck and crept down his shoulders. Had they been found out? No, that couldn't be. He was careful enough when he left, and he knew that no one would have followed them through the winding and turning passages of the caves. But where could they have gone? Did he dare call out? No, that was too risky.

Looking around, Trevian saw just the slightest movement within the wild lilacs. Oh, what sweet memories bounded to the forefront of his mind…and the longing…the longing to hold Adriena close, to feel her touch, nearly overwhelmed him as he moved in their direction.

Chapter 26

New horizon

Adriena and Serenity were talking about what they were going to do until Serenity looked up. Trevian held his hands up to keep her from saying anything in order that he might surprise Adriena. With almost a half grin from Serenity, Adriena said, "What are you smiling about?"

"Oh, I was just remembering something Darien told me a while back."

"Good, you need to smile. It is better than you being sad."

Adriena stood up a little too quickly and lost her balance. Trevian was there to catch her.

She was just a little startled, until she realized who it was, and she wasted no time throwing her arms around his neck. Then he kissed her, showing how much he'd missed her, even if only for a day. At last, they were together again! But their embrace, although impassioned, was quick. It had to be quick since time was so limited, and they needed to return to the detention cave.

Serenity cleared her throat, letting them know she was still here. Then she said, "I thought you were going to be away for a few more days or so."

"I am here quicker than I had intended. Serenity, this will not be easy for you to hear, but it is necessary before you see him. When I got there, he was barely conscious and alert. I gave him some natural

173

herbs that my father said should help if it was ever needed. I also used poultices on his open wounds to remediate the infections."

With a gasp and fighting back tears, Serenity said, "Tell me the truth. How bad is he?"

Trevian said, "Now, Serenity, calm down. It's…"

Cutting him off, she said, "Don't you dare tell me it is okay. Tell me the truth. Don't you dare hold anything back from me, please! I really need to know!"

"Serenity, I came back as fast as I could. The herbs I gave him immediately started working. He is much better than yesterday, but he is not out of the woods just yet. That is why I am here. Listen very carefully. Mr. Bonnaire told me to come back as quickly as I could to get you both. He needs us to get Darien and bring him back here. If he is to have a fighting chance, he needs no more interruptions in his getting well. He cannot take another round of discipline in punishment. Take only the medications Serenity needs, then let's go. We will be back here again soon. Hopefully before sunset. We will need to leave as much as we can here if we are to get Darien back into the caves… This will not be easy and it will be very dangerous. If we leave now, we should be able to get him back here before it gets too dark to see. Now, if you are ready, we need not waste any more time, okay?" Then he turned and picked up supplies, blankets, and packs, hiding them within the thicket of wild lilac shrubbery. As he bent over, the dark-green leaves brushed his face, and the sweet and delicate fragrance of the violet-blue blossoms brought back such wonderful memories and sensations. Was it only yesterday? So much had happened.

"Get a hold of yourself," Trevian chided himself. "There is much to do and so many lives are counting on us to get back."

Before they said anything, he looked at Serenity and said, "I need to know right now if you can do this. We may not get another chance. This is already very risky, even more so with your condition.

You know Darien will not forgive me if anything should happen to either of you. I do not want to take this chance if you are not a hundred percent sure."

"Trevian, I understand very well the risk, and I need to do this."

Cupping Adriena's face, he said, "Help me keep you and your sister safe."

"Don't worry. Serenity is a lot stronger than she looks. I promise you we will look after each other. If it is as bad as you say, let's be on our way now!"

Trevian said, "I sure hope she is, because what we see on the way back could be worse! War is getting very close to here, and nothing can prepare you for what happens on that battlefield." As if on cue, a distant "boom" could be heard.

Adriena responded to his analysis, saying, "Trevian, do you really believe it can be that bad?"

"Yes, Adriena, I do, and I want to make sure you are both protected under my watch. Now let's go, and hope to hell we don't run into anything or anyone! Also, be watchful of where and how you tread. The way we are going will be a little longer and we will do some backtracking to make it more difficult for anyone trying to track us back later. We need to be very careful not to leave a trail. Surely there will be searching for Darien once it is found out that he is missing."

They moved out with the most important items. They hurried to follow Trevian. As promised, he was careful as to where he led them. Serenity noticed that he was staying under the pines, where the needles lay in a thick carpet, and she watched as they moved how their steps seemed to disappear from sight. "He's a smart one," she thought.

The forest was fairly dense and it was only through the shifting of the sunlight as it filtered through the trees that Serenity could see the advancing of the day and the changes in direction. "How in the world does Trevian even know which way to go?" The sisters passed a marveling thought between them, understanding immediately what the other was thinking. Finally, they came to the prearranged place where Markis's men waited to escort them back to the detention cave's hidden entrance.

As they drew close to these soldiers, Serenity caught a glimpse of something out of the corner of her eye. Once they drew close enough to make out what it was, Serenity began heaving. The bloodstained figure lying in a heap near a tall pine could have been asleep, except for the wide-open eyes staring, staring into the unknown. Trevian checked for a pulse and then closed the man's eyes. There was no sign of life.

Trevian took their hands and said, "Come on, we need to hurry. Just watch your step as we proceed. There may be others who had their final battle here." He looked at Serenity, whose face had turned ashen. "Are you okay?"

"Yes, I believe so. It's been like this since I began carrying this child. I just become 'weak,' and often it doesn't take much for me to get violently ill."

Trevian said, "It could be the reason. I've seen this in others that my father has had to check on. Hopefully, there won't be other bodies. That could certainly be the reason for your discomfort. No one should have to look upon such a body. I'll ask two of the men in front to keep a lookout, and perhaps give us a warning ahead of time."

Adriena said in a whisper, "Thank you, Trevian. It should be a big help."

They continued at a fast pace, carefully watching their steps as they went. Nighttime was very close now, with just enough daylight to make it to the hidden entrance. Serenity's will was driving her to see her only love again, but her body was screaming the need to stop. The terrain had changed again, now a sandy well-worn path evidencing that many boots had recently passed. At a turn, this little group parted ways with the soft sand and stepped onto harder ground, this time firmly packed limestone. Nothing growing, just limestone; then after another quarter mile a huge meadow opened to them with nearly waist-high grasses. All of a sudden, Serenity stopped dead in her tracks, and without warning, fell to the ground. Not far ahead, Adriena sensed that something wasn't right and stopped abruptly, saying to Trevian, "Where is my sister?"

"I don't know, Adriena. She was right here a minute ago."

They retraced their steps. The sky was turning dark. The trees were now black silhouettes against a dark-gold evening sky, the beauty going unnoticed by the frantic group searching for Serenity. The grass was up to their knees here, making it difficult to see and to find Serenity. How could she have disappeared so completely? They searched frantically, careful not to give away their position.

Adriena turned in a different direction. The grass here was even deeper, and by looking at the path they had been following, she noticed that there had been a disturbance that had moved from the main group's trail. Shading her eyes from the last sun shining over the horizon, she caught just a glimpse of something moving in the grass. The ripening stalks of wild grain were moving, but not like in a breeze. She carefully walked in that direction. Just then, something grabbed her leg, startling her for just a moment, until she looked down. It was Serenity. Quietly, she motioned to Trevian, and he quickly moved to where she was.

"Trevian, it's Serenity. Her body is weak with exhaustion. We need to help her the rest of the way."

"I believe you are right, Adriena." He called for Joffery and Tallon to help her. He turned and said to Adriena, "I was afraid this would happen. I just pray she will be able to handle what Darien's been through." Gently, the two men lifted Serenity, placing her arms over their shoulders. "Serenity, can you hang on to us a bit? We will support you in this manner. Can you walk a little if we hold you up?"

"I don't know," Serenity replied weakly.

"Surely she can do this with their help. She must!"

"Trevian, I need your honest opinion. How is Darien?"

"I'm afraid, Adriena, he has a long recovery. Right now, he is exceedingly weak from all he has gone through. At least he's responding to the medications I have been able to administer. I hope she can deal with the sight of him."

"Thank you for your honesty. I'm hoping once they see each other, they both can heal. I really believe deep down this will help."

"I do hope you are right, Adriena. The alternative is not looking good for either of them right now. Now, let's get you both to safety."

Just then Alaster approached, saying, "We need to move. I've just come back from scouting our area, and the fighting is drawing closer. You'll soon hear the sounds of the advancing army. We must hurry." It seemed as if a curtain were closing on the daylight. It was now such a dark dusk that the figures were starting to blur, but one could still make out Alaster up ahead, and his associates helping Serenity, who did her best to walk with the two men supporting her. Adriena and Trevian were taking up the rear. Alaster was looking around, and just a little confused, since he couldn't see the hidden opening he had left just this morning. This was truly well hidden was his thought as they approached the area of the secret cave entrance. Only a few more steps and they arrived. The brush stood guard in front of the crevice leading into the cave. Here, each one had to squeeze themselves through the crack. It was a good thing that Serenity's body wasn't yet showing the child she carried. That could have made entering impossible for her.

Once inside, they had to light the lantern left just inside the entry earlier this morning awaiting their return. Then it was the three hundred feet back to the main part of the detention cave's hidden entrance. As they moved on, Trevian went ahead to find Markis.

"Watch after the girls, please, Alaster. Take them to the alcove at the end of this tunnel and wait there for my return. Please be sure they stay there. We cannot be found out, and I certainly don't want her to try and find Darien on her own." This was a practical and time-saving move, since Serenity was walking very slowly, still needing some help. Looking after Trevian's departing form, Adriena sighed, but stayed with her sister, knowing it was more important for Trevian to go to get Markis than for them all to come into the detention cave together.

As Trevian entered the main hall of the detention cave, he stopped first to check on Darien. Who, to his surprise, seemed to be much better than when he'd last seen him. He was sleeping peacefully, and not in the unconsciousness of this morning. Resuming his trek down the cavern's wide corridor, he wondered where he would find Markis, who then moved away from the guard, who was drinking a cup of coffee, and said, "I trust your trip was successful? If it was, where are they?"

"Yes, sir, it was! I had them brought to that small antechamber we met in yesterday. We do, however, have just a small setback. It's Serenity, sir."

"Take me to them immediately, and tell me everything that's happened while we walk."

The torches on the cavern walls flickered as the two men walked back toward the rear of the detention cavern, and then lit another lantern as they came to the small antechamber at the rear, where the girls were waiting, along with their protectors. As they walked, Trevian said, "Sir, I checked on Serenity. She will be fine. My main concern is she needs rest. This trip has been exhausting for her. I had a feeling this would happen. You need to know that Adriena did everything she could to convince her to stay. Even my medical exams wouldn't deter her from this."

"I know you did, son. I am telling you, she is her mother made over. They are both strong-willed and stubborn. As long as they have that mentality, it might be in our best interest not to push them, causing any more problems. They are, however, very smart. I will say this: use caution around them. Now, let's see how Serenity is doing, shall we?"

"Yes, sir. They should be here now."

Markis did a thorough check-up and said, "I'll have some food brought in as well as tea. That should help. There are blankets for the cots behind those curtains. I think my men can leave for now, but if things start looking risky, I'll be sure to send them back." Then Markis addressed the girls. "After eating, you should rest for the night."

Then both men left the room and proceeded back down the cavern hall to attend to Darien and to organize the promised meals. "Trevian, has Serenity been experiencing this very long?"

"No, sir, this is the first time she has passed out. I am sure that it is from exhaustion and the stress of the travel and strain of all the uncertainty…"

"Son, I sure hope you are right. We need to get them out of here as soon as possible. War is almost fully on us. Earlier, with the wind blowing from the battlefield, I thought they were already upon us. In the morning you will take a few of my men and get everyone to safety in the secret place. It is only a matter of time before Tomáš will make his appearance down here. My men know the route they must take, and then of course you need to get everyone to safety using the most circuitous route, and without evidence to lead searchers to your hiding place. Please be careful not to get split up. I'm not sure that the girls could find their way back to your special place, and Darien certainly won't be up to it. I will remain here to watch your back."

"Yes, sir, I will do as you ask. Has their mother made her way here?"

"No! She has not. My scout informed me she will be here tomorrow. I will make sure she gets back to safety as soon as I can talk some sense into her. Those girls get their stubbornness honestly from both parents, and they re very hard to reason with. You will know this soon enough. Son I know you have asked her to marry you. Are you abswolutely sure you want to do this?"

"Yes, sir. I love her very much."

"I see, and how do you plan to pull this off? Knowing my daughter-in-law, this marriage was not an easy one to pull off. I'm sure this one will be just as difficult, if not more. I should hope you have devised a plan on this! No matter, we will discuss this another time, and hopefully back in my home very soon.

"Yes, sir! I have a plan and I believe it will work."

"Trevian, I hope you are right. For now, let's focus on the task at hand. We will worry about the other later. Now go, get some needed rest tonight. I will see you in the morning at first light."

"Good night, sir."

Trevian returned to where Adriena and Serenity were eating the evening meal. They had started to nibble, but were waiting for Trevian to join them. The meager meal was set up on a small table, which was pushed up against the far wall. There was just enough room for the tray and the large teapot, which was emitting soothing chamomile aromas. Adriena was just pouring tea as Trevian entered the chamber. How beautiful she was, even with her rumpled clothes. The straggling curls bound back from her face created such a sweet backdrop for the luminous blue eyes and slightly frowning brows.

"Finally, you have returned." With the hint of a smile, Adriena continued, "We've been waiting for you while our tummies have been growling! A moment longer and there would have been nothing left for you." Both laughed as she handed him a thick slice of bread with butter. How nice to have butter and a slice of roast from last night's meal here in the compound. There was also cheese and some slices of sausage, figs, and two apples. The cavern was surprisingly warm. It must have been all the body heat. By lantern light, they sat on the cots, Adriena and Trevian together with Serenity across.

"When can I see Darien?" Serenity queried. She was quieted now, just knowing he was close by, but worry creased her brow as she remembered Trevian's words when they'd started their trek to the detention cave. A queasy feeling started in her tummy. How was he? Then it settled again as she relaxed, knowing he was close and that soon they would be together again.

After thoughtfully chewing and a last swallow, Trevian replied, "Tomorrow morning. I will take you to him tomorrow. Tonight you need to rest and sleep. This tea should help to relax you. Sure is working for me! But seriously, tomorrow will be a strenuous day. We will all be leaving to return to your safe caverns. It will likely be difficult. We may need to avoid combatants as well as our own forces, whom we don't want to encounter. The battles are drawing closer, so we will need to leave early. Morning will come soon. Let's extinguish the lanterns now and leave only a small candle. Anyone needing to relieve themselves may go to the latrine. I'm sorry, but it is only a bucket. But at least Alaster has brought one for just you girls. You will find it in a smaller niche just to the left of this chamber. I also asked him to bring a couple of pitchers of water, a bowl, and clean towels so you might freshen up a bit." With that, Trevian excused himself to go sleep with the rest of the men at the head of the cavern.

Chapter 27

Perlious Journey

Before daybreak, Serenity woke in a jolt. Barely making it to the corridor of the cave, she began heaving. Adriena ran to her sister to help her, until it finally subsided. She made the special drink and lifted the cup to Serenity's quivering lips. After about thirty minutes, she washed up, using the last of the water left in the pitchers. She was grateful for Trevian's thoughtfulness for bringing the water and proceeded to straighten her outfit.

Serenity quickly moved toward Darien and sat beside him, caressing his face with both her hands.

Adriena said, "Serenity, are you sure you're up to this? You need more rest!"

"I'm sorry, Adriena, I must see Darien. I can wait no longer."

"I understand, but you really need to rest a little longer," Adriena said, moving her long black hair out of her eyes and noticing the sadness within the eyes of her sister. "I can see I can't change your mind, so if you insist, I insist on walking with you."

Serenity hugged her sister and agreed to her words. They walked together down the corridor, encountering Trevian. "I was just coming to get you. Come quickly, you cannot be discovered by the guards. Darien is in this room." He turned the key and opened the detention-room door. Serenity quickly moved toward Darien and sat behind him, caressing his face with both her hands. Quietly, she said,

"What have they done to you?" He began to stir and she made sure it was her face he saw as his eyes began to open.

In a dramatic long-awaited scene, his eyes fixed upon the one he loved. He said, "Am I dreaming?"

"No, my love, I am here and I'll never leave your side."

Weak and heavy-laden, he said softly "How—how did you find me?" Serenity shushed him with a kiss. Breaking from the hold, he said, "You should not be here. This is very dangerous and you should not have come."

"I'm sorry, Darien, but I cannot stand idly by with what my father is doing to you. When your father said we had one chance, one window to free you, I had to come. I'm begging you to take this window of opportunity and leave with me." While he shook his head no, she shushed him once more. "If not for yourself, do this for us! I need you desperately. I cannot do this. I cannot have this child without you!" she said as tears welled and spilled down her cheeks. With every aching bone in his body, he mustered his strength, lifting his hand to her face, wiping her tears. Beaten nearly to death, he'd almost forgotten what he'd left behind.

His father came to check on them, and said, "Son, you have only this chance to be freed from this hell. I suggest you take it."

Darien said, "What about her father? He'll hunt me down!"

"Yes, Son, he will try, but he will not succeed. I will make sure of it. Where you go, you'll both be safe. Know that her father shared with me to do this when we were able to speak alone. When we are all safe again once more I will explain more, but for now, I need you to muster all the strength you have, and run where my men will take you." Lifting his son's eyes to his, he said, "Now, Son! We need to hurry!"

Adriena heard something, and Trevian ran as fast as he could from the entrance to meet them. Almost out of breath, he said,

"Serenity! Adriena! You need to hurry. Get him out of here now! No time to explain! Your father is on his way!"

Markis helped Serenity with Darien, rushing to get them to safety. Darien was barely moving, yet mustering all the meager strength he could as they made their way to Alaster and the men escorting them the way they needed to go.

Trevian said, "You go! I will stay behind and buy you some time."

Adriena looked at her sister and said, "Go. I can handle our father."

"No! Adriena, you can't. You need to come with us."

"Don't worry, Serenity, I promise you, I will be fine. Besides, I'm in good hands," she said as she looked at Trevian.

Trevian looked at her and said, "Very well, on one condition. You listen and do as I say. I mean it. Your safety is first and foremost."

Adriena looked at him and said, "I will listen."

Trevian took Adriena by the hand and led her back into the secret entrance. He said, "I need you to stay here where you were. I have to run to the entrance before your father walks through. Need to time it all perfectly. I will return when it is clear."

Adriena began to say something, but Trevian shushed her not to utter a word. He looked her directly in the eyes and said, as he cupped her face, "I promise you, I will return as quickly as I can. Trust me." He kissed her tenderly and said, "I can't lose you now that I've found the one I love. Besides, we have a wedding to plan. Now stay here and be very quiet. I will be back as soon as I possibly can. Promise not to take off!"

"I will wait and promise not to leave. Whatever you do, handle Father quickly before he has a chance to think things through," she said with a smile.

Nodding his head in agreement, he ran outside to meet her father at the entrance, barely making it before he went in.

Tomáš said, "Son, what brings you here this early?"

"Sir, I got word to come check on Darien and to give him a special mix to help him heal quicker. I ask for your approval to do so."

"Yes, Son, I will grant it. Though it will do no good. I'm afraid my superiors have sentenced him to be executed at first light tomorrow. I am on my way to give his father this information personally and let him know of his rights and find out his wishes before this happens."

"But, sir! Is there no other way? He needs to be with his wife and unborn child. I'm afraid she may not make it through this without him."

"Son, are you completely certain of this?"

"Yes, sir, my father has told me so! She is alone, and even your wife knows this to be true. Ask her if you don't believe me. Please, sir, let him go!"

"Trevian, I will think on your words for now. If what you say is true, I will ask Arabel. Until then, let's go check on him."

Trevian was playing it cool, not knowing what to expect when Tomáš saw Darien was not there.

They walked quickly to where Darien was supposed to be. As Tomáš approached, he saw the door was unlocked.

Surveying the empty room, Tomáš sprang into action, saying, "Guards! Search the grounds immediately! He couldn't have gone far!"

He turned to Trevian and said, "Do you know anything about this?"

"No, sir! You saw yourself, I just got here myself."

"Trevian! Where is your father?"

"He was at home when I was told to come here to check on things for him. Sir! If I may? What is going on?"

"Trevian, I will say this once, and do not pursue for more information. Am I clear?"

"Yes, sir!"

"My superiors gave the orders that he is to be executed. If I find anyone that aided in his release, they will serve a swift and painful punishment. Son, I pray you are not any part of this at all." He leaned forward with an angry look upon his face, and said, "Because, Son, if you are found guilty, your punishment will be swift and painful unlike any you've ever felt. Do I make myself clear?!"

"Yes, sir! Loud and clear. Sir, if I may, I wish to return to my father. May I return?"

"I'll grant your leave to return, and I must insist on an escort of my personal men. Is this understood?"

"Yes, sir! If I may be permitted to gather my medical supplies, I'll then be on my way."

"Very well, Trevian, you have one hour. I suggest you make haste and quickly ready yourself."

"Thank you, I will not let you down."

Then Tomáš leaned in with one more thing to say. "Son, for your sake, you had better not!"

"Thank you, sir!"

Tomáš took his men outside to begin searching every inch of the place. As soon as he got away, Trevian ran to Adriena and gathered everything he had, and extra supplies to give to Adriena, sending her to catch up with Serenity.

"Adriena, I need you to hurry to that secret entrance. Those men will guard your life. Please! Don't stop," he said, kissing her quickly.

"What about you? I can't leave you!'

"Adriena, please! I don't have much time. His men will be escorting me back to my home." She had tears streaming down her face. He wiped them away and kissed her as he held her in a warm embrace. "Please, Adriena, I will find you. I know a secret passage from my home. It may take me longer to reach. I promise, I will find you. My father will make sure of it."

He took her to the cracked entrance they had just entered through the night before and waited for his men to confirm the coast was clear. They hurriedly took Adriena, cloaked in their midst. She appeared to be one of them as they guided her down the long tunnel. After watching her figure fade, he raced to get his belongings and meet his escort to go home. Carefully, he said as little as possible, mostly not to give away anything that would set them on his trail. He had half a day's ride ahead of him.

Chapter 28

Miscalculation

Adriena returned to the secret entrance. Desperately, she looked for her sister. Her only entrance to this path had been in the darkness, and she had been so exhausted she had not really paid attention. She was going "along" with those who knew. Now unsure, she followed a path that her sister seemed to have taken. She came to a place where the path divided. Had it divided before? She didn't remember. It seemed as though it had all just gone one way.

Trying to collect her thoughts, Adriena took a deep breath. "Which do I take?" She hurried along, trying to catch up, assuming that her sister's party was just up ahead. Surely they could not be far. Neither Serenity nor Darien were so strong as to move very fast and maintain that speed. After walking a few more steps, she realized something was wrong. After noticing that she hadn't been here before, Adriena turned around and headed back to the divided path. She stopped to rest for a little bit, and took a drink of water before she continued, grateful that Trevian had provided her with a flask as well as some of the ham-and-cheese breakfast rolls. They hadn't eaten before Serenity's persistence to see Darien in the holding cell––even though they had breakfast waiting for them in the antechamber, left untouched. Her thoughts drifted to her fiance, wondering where he was and when she would see him again. She now knew how difficult separation from a soul mate and beloved could be, just as her sister did. Adriena pushed her thoughts aside so she could continue to make her way swiftly back to her sister. Now wasn't the time to ruminate on the wonderful feelings that assailed her when in Trevian's presence, or to speculate when she would again see him and under what circumstances. She said to herself, "I need to keep my thoughts on track. I have to find my sister. Serenity, where are you? Please tell me I am getting close to finding you!"

As Adriena continued to look for her sister, she looked at every turn, hoping for a few clues here and there. At a distance, she heard voices echoing through the cave, could that be them? She listened more intently. She followed the sounds until she was almost upon them. Her heart pounding fiercely, Adriena looked at her surroundings. "No, this doesn't look right." Quietly, she retraced her steps, careful not to give away her position. She went back to where she'd started, and noticed something her sister had left. What she found contained writing in the hand of Serenity. This note provided directions for her to follow and said, "Adriena, if you are reading this, take the next left, then a right. There you will find me. Read into my thoughts as you read this. You will understand."

Adriena knew this meant to go into the opposite direction than what was written. This was a double safe note, since the sisters had developed their own form of communicating and even writing as girls. It was a fun game for them, knowing neither friends nor parents could decipher the intent of their scribbled notes. Now the secret writing, along with their deep understanding of one another, would keep them safe.

Markis looked at Serenity while Darien was resting and said, "You know, my dear, you should try and get some rest. You will see your sister again. I know Adriena is very smart and she will stop at nothing to find you."

"I know, sir. I can't help but wonder where she is. I worry for her and Trevian. I worry for my love and that he too should be okay. All I can say is, I will try." Caressing Darien's forehead, she said, "Do you think he is at all aware I am here?"

"Honestly, Serenity, we will know soon enough. I do know that what Trevian gave Darien is an ancient remedy, but even to this day, it has been proven to be effective. Besides, he is responding as he should with this, and that should be of comfort to you."

"Perhaps you're right, sir. I still worry."

"Serenity, please try to sleep while we finally have a short resting time here. You will do no good for him being exhausted."

Finally making her way to them, Adriena heard the last advice Markis gave to Serenity as she silently moved into their presence. He looked up just as she motioned for silence. He just smiled and carried on.

With a smile in her voice, Adriena picked up Markis's admonitions. "Serenity, he is right, you know! You need rest." A smile so bright as to light the darkness of the tunnel broke across Serenity's face at her sister's words.

Gently laying Darien's head down on a folded jacket, she stood to embrace her sister. "Adriena! You made it! Where's Trevian? I thought you would be together!"

"Serenity, we were, but he needed to create a diversion. He led our father toward him in helping me to reach you. We had no choice. He is going to warn his father and make his way to us as soon as he can."

"Oh, Adriena, I'm so sorry it happened this way!"

"It's okay, Serenity. I have faith I will see him again. I just don't know when, which brings me to my next point. I believe a few of Father's men have followed me. I tried to mask the trail to keep them from finding us. I hope what I did will be good enough." She

191

explained to Markis what she had done, and in that moment they heard violent screams.

Markis raised his eyebrows and said, "Sounds as if it is working. We may need to go to the next place just to be on the safe side. We must quickly get moving."

"Is it safe enough to move Darien? I mean, he is sleeping."

Markis, looking at them both, said, "We have no choice. The quicker we can get there, the better we will be. Let's move quietly."

Not a word as they began the journey. Markis said in a whisper, "It should only take us a couple of hours to get there." He led, helping Darien along the way, while Adriena helped her sister. Alaster returned from scouting ahead with fresh lanterns that had been stored for just such a time, providing them much-needed lighting. Joffrey and Tallon were moving cautiously with heavy backpacks, lugging food and water with blankets distributed evenly between themselves. Their firearms hung comfortingly along their sides, and the bandoleer-style bullet packs hearkened back to another era.

Chapter 29

Treacherous Path

About an hour into their walk, Markis said, "Girls, heed this warning. The path I'm taking lies just ahead. Watch your step carefully. It is a dangerous and treacherous path. Stay as close to the wall as you possibly can and you will make it through this. Please! I can't stress it enough, watch your steps closely. I'm going to need to wake Darien. I hope he will be strong enough." Then he turned to Alaster. "Please come assist me with Darien. I need to fully wake him now, so that he will not endanger himself or us as we come to this difficult crossing on the thin ledge." Then to himself he thought, "I hope he can endure this and last the hour it will take to cross."

Serenity said, "Sir, how are you going to get Darien to listen! He can barely stand!"

"Serenity, the remedy Trevian gave him has helped him rest. Once I wake him, we must move quickly. With Alaster's help, he should have enough energy to do this. It is the only chance we have. We needed to take this alternate route to the secret caves, since your father has all the area crawling with soldiers looking for you. Now we must hurry."

While he was still speaking, he was pulling coiled rope from a recess in the dark sloping cavern wall. "There are three big ledges across this huge ravine that has to be crossed. You'll not want to look

193

down as we move along the narrow path along the side of the cavern. The path is safe enough, as long as you place your feet very carefully and concentrate on how you move. At the end of each narrow ledge path we will come onto a wide ledge where we can stop to rest. These ledges are wide enough to relax without fear of a slip or a fall. They are also around bends in the cavern, so as not to be visible to prying or searching eyes. But it is incredibly important that we cross at least the very first of such ledges before the searchers are upon us. We cannot stay for long. Now we must hurry. Here, tie this rope around your waist, not too tight but comfortably. I will run the rope through the slots to help guide us along the way. Alaster, when you pass each last slot, remove the slot ring so no one coming behind us has access to these pins. Now, are you ready?"

Serenity looked at Darien one more time before he woke and nodded her head yes in reply.

Markis put the smelling salts under his son's nose. Darien stirred, waking. Markis took his son's head in his hand, forcing Darien to look at him. He said, "Son, look at me. I need you to focus. I don't have the time to explain. We need to cross this path as quickly as we can, so that we are not followed. Are you strong enough to do this? I need you to stand now!"

Darien stood as he was asked. He proceeded with caution. He noticed his love, Serenity, and embraced her closely as his father said, "Come, let's move. We need to cross this great cavern. There will be plenty of time for this later." Reluctantly releasing Serenity, he nodded his head yes in reply.

"But, Father! She's with child! How are we to make it on this narrow path?!"

"Son, trust me! She can do this. She has to. We have no choice."

Serenity turned Darien's face to hers. Looking deeply into his eyes, she said as she cupped his face, "It's okay, I can do this."

He took her hand to his lips and kissed it, and ran his fingers down the slight bulge of her belly, feeling the warmth of her body and the child she was carrying. Then, as he looked deeply into her eyes, he said, "Then we do this together, the three of us," and gave her a weak smile.

Joffrey headed out first, adjusting his pack for better balance. First one step, then another. Markis came next, then Darien with Serenity behind. Adriena, watching her sister's steps as closely as her own, noticed how Darien's strength had returned and how focused he was on Serenity's crossing. "Good," she thought, "he has regained his strength and is being strong for his love." Tallon, with his pack, was only one or two steps behind Adriena, with Alaster bringing up the rear. The crossing on this ledge was made more difficult, since they only had three lanterns between them, making the path difficult to see. Joffrey carried the first, Markis the second, and Tallon the third, lighting both for Adriena and for Alaster, so he could pull the rings. Each person carefully shuffled along, trailing one hand on the wall of the cavern, and holding on to even the smallest rocky outcropping. They moved carefully to the first ledge, and then caught their breath while they rested. It had been a difficult yet uneventful crossing. "I saw no one at the trailhead as I pulled the last ring to round this corner," reported Alaster to Markis as they shared the water flask and flexed their rigid and strained muscles. Darien rubbed Serenity's neck, where the tension of the last half hour had settled.

After a fifteen-minute rest, Markis urged them on. "It's time we got going again. I know this has been a short rest, but we are not out of danger. Our pursuers will likely be making their way here now, so we must move on. This second stretch will be a bit uphill, and is still a very, very narrow trail. To our benefit, the cavern walls slope slightly away from the crevasse, so we can lean in a bit. That will help. However, I must warn you there are a few places where the path has fallen off and we must jump across. Don't worry about that now, just know it will come up, and we will be very careful to get across."

They continued on to the next narrow ledge, leaning in just as Markis had suggested. It wasn't long before the party came to a halt as Joffrey indicated that they had come to a section where the path was gone. The hard granite had deteriorated into a more granular limestone, where water or some careless soul had misstepped and broken the narrow trail into nothingness. Joffrey juggled his pack once again for balance, then, holding lightly onto the wall with his left hand and stretching out his right hand with the lantern, took a long step onto the other side. He proceeded along the path for a few feet and set his pack down along with the lantern. Joffrey unwrapped the rope from around his waist so that he could hold on to the rope that was tethered along the wall for support. He assisted Markis to the ledge and proceeded to help the rest one by one to cross. After Tallon tossed his pack and lantern across to Joffrey, he jumped across. Alaster came last, also handing the pack and lantern off first before his jump to the narrow path. On the way back Joffrey assisted Alaster, to help him cross the corroded ledge. As Joffrey stood on the edge he held out his hand for Alaster, and helped him cross. Joffrey released the pin from the wall and the corrosion gave way under his foot. He reached trying to grab anything to hold onto but nothing was there. Alaster could not get to him quick enough. In just a few seconds he fell to his death. Joffrey was gone in an instant and everyone was so stunned the look of shock on their face they could not comprehend what they just witnessed. They had no choice and had to move on.

It was only a few feet before the path broadened into a wide ledge. This ledge was four times as wide as the previous ledge and twice as long. It appeared to have been a watch "tower" or place for a long-gone race. There were hollows that appeared to have been sleeping ledges, and also an area that held the remains of cooking fires beneath a natural chimney opening to the sky. It was now apparent that the day was getting long. At the loss of their friend, everyone said a silent prayer in remembrance of Joffrey's memory. The noonday sun had traveled on, and the weary company noticed the gnawing of hunger in their tummies. Tallon unpacked the bundle of sandwiches and passed around the water flask for sustenance while they gave their weary muscles a well-deserved rest. Everyone was tired, but Serenity, who was halfway through her second trimester, was exhausted. Fatigue was setting in. Fatigue that she would not allow. No, she had to be strong.

Markis looked at them all, and said, "This will be the hardest part yet. Please be very careful and do not take the rope from your waist for any reason whatsoever!" The path once again narrowed as they left the broad ledge, and seemed to get impossibly thin.

"How are we to navigate this?" wondered Adriena as the dimming light, now again back to lantern light, revealed the hazardous path. She remembered Markis's words from earlier: "We have to get around the last corner to be completely safe." Silently, she wondered how it would be possible to be "completely safe."

"Not much farther now, we can do this," called out Markis to encourage the weary group, while thanking God that Darien had regained his strength and was even able to assist Serenity. It was as he had hoped, and he was ever so grateful to the good Lord and to Trevian's herbal solution.

They began to move forward. Serenity was rounding the corner with her back up against the cavern wall, grateful that here too the slope was inward, making it easier to slide herself these last difficult steps toward safety. Beads of water began to form on her forehead, right before a pain set in. She completely stopped as if paralyzed, leaning against the wall, gasping for air. Before her was a long drop into the seemingly bottomless crevasse. She fought to regain her steps.

Darien turned around as he noticed the pull on the rope. Something was wrong. Serenity was pale and gasping for air. He reached out to her, realizing that she was in the clutches of pain. The why was concerning, but the situation at hand, and the location on this precariously narrow path, could have horrifying consequences. He grabbed her hand and the rope. "I've got you, take it slowly! You can do this! Just a few more steps." Markis reached to help as she drew closer onto the now widening ledge. Adriena looked on in worrisome concern. Oh, how could this be happening now?

Markis said, "Come on, Serenity! That's it. Almost there! You can do this!" Finally able to reach for her other hand, he helped Darien pull her to safety, and turned to Adriena to say, "Quickly, hand me the medical bag."

Adriena, just able to squeeze around the trio, said, "What's happening?"

"We need to stop her contractions. She is not ready. It is too early for this baby to come."

Adriena said, "Here's the bag. What can I do to help?"

"Hand me the syringe and that vial marked Xlotuimnum." He pointed. "This will slow down the contractions and help Serenity to relax. As soon as she is stable, we need to get her to a bed, and she is to remain there until it is time."

"My sister can be very stubborn with this."

"Adriena, I'm well aware of her stubbornness," Markis said with a shake of his head and an exasperated look on his face. "Both of you take after your mother in that respect. We need to convince her otherwise. Right now, let's just concentrate on stopping this, and on getting to your safe hiding place."

Darien rubbed Serenity's forehead as Markis said, "Sweetheart, I need you to listen. I'm going to give you something to ease the pain and hopefully stop it. The downside to this is it will make you sleepy. Now, you need not worry, we will get you to where we are going. It will be much easier to get you there."

Darien looked at Serenity and kissed her as he said, "Don't worry. My father knows what he is doing. Everything will be fine. I'm right here. I promise, I'm not going anywhere."

Not able to say anything at the moment, she shook her head in acknowledgment.

After they gave her the shot, she began to relax with the voices fading more.

Markis said to Serenity, "Relax, you will be fine, Serenity."

She looked at Darien one last time as she closed her eyes.

Once she was asleep, he looked at his father and said, "I hope this works."

"Me too, Son. She is so exhausted and hasn't been able to rest. I'm afraid that is what brought this on. She needs to be very careful and take it easy. Trevian was concerned that this could happen, and it is for this reason that he provided me with his extra medical bag, the medicine, and syringe. I am so grateful for his foresight. What an extraordinary young man. I can only pray that all goes well for him with Tomáš. Now, we need to keep her as stress-free as possible under these circumstances. I want her delivery to be as easy as we can make it when the time comes."

Darien said, "Father? Where are you taking us?"

"Son, I prepared a special place for you to live without any interruption, and if God is willing, to raise your family. Only a few will know this location, and they are whom I trust the most. I believe you will both be very happy here. You both need to rest with no more separation, and this will give it to you."

"I understand, Father, I will listen. I cannot stand to be away from her. I need her as much as she needs me."

"Darien? Are you strong enough to carry her, or shall I?"

"I can do this, Father. Lead the way, so we can follow."

Markis said as he held out his arm, "Very well, Son. Adriena? Shall we?"

Chapter 30

Breaking Point

After a few steps, a lightly muffled sound reached their ears. It was the mini explosions Alaster had set along the last narrow ledge culminating at the last turn. Now the "holes" in the path were so wide that no followers could continue their path to catch them. They would have to turn back or die.

The now-invigorated group continued the treacherous journey down the stony path, going through huge chasms within the cave, Darien carrying Serenity, who felt light in his strong arms. Who would have thought that he would be carrying mother and child? How precious his burden, really no burden at all. Because of his love, his brain did not perceive the burning in the muscles of his arms, nor the pull on his hamstrings as he stumbled on the rocks covering sections of path. "At least this path is wide and we have left those deadly crevasses," he thought.

Occasionally now, some areas of these caverns, which were as high as the crevasses were low, opened to the blue sky above. The sun seeping through a light canopy of fringed trees was a delightful surprise to this group of travelers. Finally out of the darkness, they had stowed the lanterns and were enjoying natural daylight. Now the sun was sending its warming presence to break the cold that had been their constant companion.

Darien said to Markis, "Father? This looks familiar. It's like I've been here before."

"You have been here, Son. Though you were very young; I didn't think you would remember it."

"If I remember correctly, it seems there are some cascading falls nearby. I can hear them now."

"Seems you do remember and are very observant. Though I did not expect you to remember. Okay, it looks like we are finally here. Let me show you around so you can be more familiar with your surroundings. First, Darien, I need you to bring Serenity, so she can rest comfortably."

Darien followed to see where his father was taking them. They came to a chamber with a king-size bed. Years in the making, Markis had made a secured place to live and enhanced a cave leading back to his home. The bed had four posters and heavy curtains, which were tied back. The curtains were both for privacy and for warmth in the night.

"Now, Darien," his father said. "This is one of the finest there is made. I need you to lay Serenity here and let me show you and Adriena around."

Darien did as asked and gently laid Serenity down without disturbing her sleep.

Markis led them on a short tour of the cavern. The ceilings were high and the walls were covered with beautiful tapestries, bringing warmth to the otherwise cold walls. These wall hangings were beautifully made, almost looking like paintings, and made one think that there were windows.

"How delighted Serenity will be when she sees these" went through Adriana's mind.

"Darien, you will find a couple of bathrooms here. I had thought that perhaps more than one family might be living here, so there is plenty of room for you here, as well Adriena. There is full running

201

water brought in from the falls outside. Everything a home can provide is here." He took them to another area, pointing above them, saying, "There's your cascading waterfall. You have plenty of food, and more provisions will be brought in as you need, and to replenish what has already been stored up for you. Now, take time to rest yourselves. Adriena, here are your rooms. I hope you like them."

As Adriena stepped through the opening to her new personal space, she was amazed at her reactions. The room was lovely. Creamy walls with tapestries giving her a beautiful sense of walled gardens and forests with deer and wild turkeys. The stitching was so fine that it appeared to be painted. A small washstand was in one corner, and the two large armchairs stood in the other. This room also had a large king-size four-poster bed with similar heavy curtains, only this bed had built-in drawers in the base. Upon further exploration, Adriena found two of the drawers contained extra linens, blankets, and pillows. A pleasant surprise was the soft downy comforter and a fluffy baffled feather bed. The sound of Markis's voice coming from the hall brought her back to the present.

"I will send word when it is clear, and you can come to the house again. Right now, this is the safest place to be. Please be careful, Son."

Adriena said, "Will you send word letting me know when and if you hear from Trevian? I am so worried about him."

Wiping the tears from her eyes, Markis said, "Don't worry over this. I will make it a priority to find his whereabouts, and I will get him here as quickly as I can. I promise to do my best. Besides, he is a very smart young man and I'm sure he will come to the house as quickly as he can. If anyone needs to be here, he does. I need someone to help deliver this baby when it is time."

Lightening the mood with a light chuckle, he walked them to the kitchen and introduced them to Michiko and Stefan, two of his trusted servants. "Welcome, welcome," they said with wide smiles. "We have been waiting, and will fix you a good meal."

Before Markis left, he said, "By the way, I have stocked some clothing here for you. Adriena, there is enough for you and Serenity to share…and, well, I suppose Serenity will not be able to wear many of these for a while. So until we can get your clothes here, I suppose these will do. You'll find the clothes in the bedroom closet."

Darien helped Serenity from the bed and to the table, joining them in the wonderful hot dinner provided by their new friends Michiko and Stefan.

Darien said to Serenity, while looking at his father, "My father said he will bring Trevian as soon as he can to monitor you and help me continue to heal." Looking deeply into her eyes with great concern, he continued, "He said you need to relax, and I agree with him." Taking her hand in his, he said, "We are in a very safe place. He will make sure we are provided with everything we need. I intend to enjoy every minute with you in this home and welcoming our new baby when it comes. Being away from you was pure torture, and I will not let that happen again. You and our family mean more to me than life itself." He looked at his father, smiling as he said, "Thank you."

Markis looked at them directly. With comforting words, he said while smiling, "My son is right. You have nothing to worry about. You are safe. I know this is a bit of an adjustment, but you will learn to cope with all things in time. Michiko and Stefan are some of my most loyal servants. They will help with whatever is necessary." He kissed Serenity's hand after the meal.

Markis looked at Adriena with great concern and said, "Please make sure your sister is not left alone. You know as well as I your sister needs to be carefully watched until the baby is born. Do you understand?"

"Yes, sir! I understand, Mr. Bonnaire. She will be."

As he looked directly at Serenity, he said, "I mean it, no more adventures like this last one, understood?"

"Yes, sir, I promise, I will listen. I don't want to jeopardize any more than I already have," she said as she looked at Darien with a smile.

As soon as they finished, Markis returned home. He took a different route home, this time through the forest, and then back into the cavern through a well-hidden narrow opening to wait for Trevian's arrival. He knew Tomáš would be hot on Trevian's trail until Arabel could intercept him and alter his course. That was what he hoped she could do, at least long enough for Trevian to reach his father and fill him in.

Now Markis, walking with only Alaster, felt his years. It had been long days for a week now, and the last two days just seemed unending. One hour ran into the next. He had to plan, execute, and be strong for his son, the girls, and of course his unborn grandchild. He was happy that he wasn't traveling alone. Having Alaster at his side helped him keep his steps moving along through the darkened tunnel. He was drained. It helped to have Alaster leading the way. For the first time, he could just put one foot in front of the other. His bed called him, but that was still a long ways away.

He thought of Joffery and Tallon, whom he had left with the young people. These five people were his most trusted servants. Yes, more than servants. They had been with him for several years, and Michiko and Stefan counted Joffery and Tallon as "dads." Markis had taken them in to live on a house on his property. It only made sense that Michiko and Stefan marry, and they were excited to help with the renovation and furnishing of the cavern home for Darien and Serenity. This had been quite a project, and keeping it secret had been of utmost importance. Markis marveled at how things had worked out to be mutually beneficial. Never would he have thought when they were kids that they would one day be caring for his son and family. Amazing how life could take turns. But then, he knew how difficult it was to raise a motherless child.

Arabel intercepted Tomáš in the tree-studded meadow. If he hadn't had a heads-up from his old friend Markis, he would have been caught completely off guard. As it was, he had been turning over and over in his mind this meeting with Arabel. Oh, how he loved this woman. She had been the abiding love in his life. It was thoughts of Arabel that brought him home out of the last war. It was indescribably difficult, and had nearly destroyed him. But it was Arabel's loving letters that came through to his command from time to time, and the palpable love that he could always––even now––"feel" that brought him through. Yes, she had loved another before him. She had loved Markis. But since her father thought Tomáš a better match, there was no choice for Arabel. She could not disobey her father, no matter what her heart wanted. Tomáš recognized this from the beginning. Arabel learned to love him. Tomáš knew that she loved him as deeply as she had loved Markis. What bothered him was how that last war had nearly killed him. Not just him physically…but killed his soul. If he hadn't had Arabel and the girls to return home to, he would have been a lost man. A lost soul.

Now the sight of his beloved wife brought him to a halt. "Tomáš! I need you to stop. Please stop."

With feigned anger, he said, "Arabel! Go home! You shouldn't be here! It is too dangerous for you! Please, go home," he pled. Knowing that Arabel came for a compelling reason, and not wanting to acknowledge the darkness that had been haunting him once again, and knowing that Arabel would see right through his bravado, he turned his face from his wife.

"Tomáš! You know as well as I that I can't go home. Not now with so much at stake. One is concerning our daughter, Serenity! Please, Tomáš, hear what I have to say!"

Tomáš halted his men just to hear what his wife needed to say. While in a safe territory, he gave the order to make camp, and they pitched a tent so he could talk to his wife alone.

"Arabel, this had better be worth my time. You know that this war is nearly upon us. Can't you hear the fighting in the distance? My orders are to advance to the front and not to dally."

Arabel cut Tomáš off, not knowing the outcome, since she had never done this before. In a voice bordering on tears, she said, "Tomáš, please listen to me." With his full attention, she continued, "Tomáš, I would love to return home, but it is no longer safe there. I know you don't want to hear the rest of what I need to say, but I beg you to please listen..."

Tomáš was moved by Arabel's approach. He had rarely seen her so forceful and determined and at the same time so moved, so broken. "Very well, Arabel, tell me quickly."

Nodding her head with acceptance, she continued, "First, your friend Markis has graciously offered for me to stay in his home until the war is over."

"No! Absolutely not! I will not, and I cannot accept this!" he scolded her with a frown on his face. But hadn't he suggested just this approach to Markis a few days ago? He wanted Arabel safe and knew that Markis would do just that. But now, faced with the suggestion coming from Arabel...it brought out the fear and jealousy that he always felt when the three of them were in the same room. He knew that Arabel loved him, but always was aware that Markis was her first love...

Cupping his face to calm him, she said, "You promised to listen." After he looked into her warm and loving eyes, he agreed for her to continue. "Now, you know full well I would not do this without reasons behind it. First, our daughter is expecting our first grandchild. I believe Markis may already have told you, but if not, you need to hear it now from me. She is in a very delicate condition and needs the best care she can get. She and her baby, our grandchild, are under tremendous distress. She needs Trevian to be there as her personal physician. His father has already said he will accompany you as the physician for your troops. You know I need to be there for our daughter. I do not make light of the request. I only ask for your consent. This is the only reason I ask. Please allow this and permit me to be there. My loyalty lies with you, and you know how much I love you. Please! I beg you to let me be there for our daughter!"

The tears that had been threatening now started to roll down Arabel's cheeks in earnest. Tomáš pulled her close and said as he lifted her eyes to his, "Arabel, you know I don't like this one bit. I will put aside our differences and allow this for the sake of our daughter." Arabel understood; even without words she had always known that this strong man, this mighty warrior, always felt a little at a loss when he thought of her previous relationship with Markis. She could understand that her living under the same roof with Markis while Tomáš was off immersed in this incredible war would be a bit unnerving for him.

A hard expression took over his countenance as he said, "Arabel, you will do well not to use this tone with me again. Remember that." Then, softening his demeanor, he said, "Now, I will have my men escort you to Markis in the morning. I shall have one night with my wife before you go." This he said with a devious smile and a quick wink. Then he picked her up without warning and took her into his tent.

"It's been too long since I've held you in my arms, Arabel. I loved you then, I love you still. I wish the war to be over and for us to be a family again as it used to be. I wished that we could go home together and be there with our daughter and Darien to welcome our first grandchild into the world." Kissing her while caressing her face, he said, "Please tell our girls how much I do love them. I will try not to let the madness overwhelm me. I promise you I will fight it. If it should overtake me, I ask for your forgiveness. Though I do not like you staying at the Bonnaire residence, please tell my old friend that I do appreciate all he does for my family. I am in his debt for all that he has done on my behalf."

He snuggled into her well-developed bosom, feeling the heaving of every breath, and smelling the wonderful womanly aromas that always accompanied his wife. Yes, she was his wife. The woman who had borne his two daughters. What a difficult delivery that had been, and how surprised they were to have been blessed with two! He had hoped for a son, but there were no more children. Perhaps it had to do with the first war and his obsession during that conflict. Their relationship just wasn't the same. He felt her love, but he himself felt less worthy, and sought to drown himself in work. Developing their homestead, increasing the size of their holdings and their standing in the community. Somehow he had never felt worthy of this woman after all that he had done and seen in that awful conflict. It was that feeling that had built a barrier between them, and then between him and the girls as they grew older.

Now, as he lay at her side, exhausted from the loving they had had, almost as in their younger days, he wondered if he could ever get it turned around and come back to being his "old" self––that younger Tomáš. With a sigh, he thought that would probably be unlikely, since he was headed back into war, and truly didn't know if the darkness would this time overcome him. Well, if it did, he knew that Markis would take care of Arabel. Somehow, this was not a comfort, and caused him to bristle.

For now, he relaxed, feeling the heartbeat of his wife and only sweetheart. This was enough for him now. He vowed to himself to do all he could to make it through this conflict and to shield his heart from the savages of war. Yes, there were orders he had to follow, and there were those that were only too eager to point out any reluctance he had in following those orders. But he knew he would have to make and maintain a safe space for himself, his inner self, or he would not come back from this conflict as a whole man. As a man his wife and daughters could love. He pulled Arabel close once again, and even in her sleep, she snuggled closer, sensing his need and his complete and abiding love for her.

Chapter 31

Overseen

Trevian hurried up the trail, stumbling a bit due to fatigue and speed, hoping his father was there and that he would understand. "Dad?" he called out. "Dad, where are you?"

"I'm here, in the stables. It's time for me to join the troops and I was just getting ready to saddle my horse."

"Father! Tomáš comes for you with great need!"

"What happened, Son? Slow down, take your time."

Trevian slowed his breathing and his father said, "Good. Now tell me what you are muttering about."

"Father, Tomáš comes for us. Markis took his son, Darien, away from his clutches."

"Why would he attempt this deed, knowing this will be of no good to anyone?"

"Father, Darien needed to be away from there. He was getting so much worse, and the torture 'punishment' was continuing. Markis went to see for himself. He told me to hurry and get you, as I am to return to his residence and help Serenity. Then, as he and Darien and the girls fled, I went to Tomáš to be a distraction. At that time Tomáš told me that the high command had ordered an execution for Darien the next morning. It was a saving grace that they had already left through a secret passage. Father, I pray Serenity is better once she sees Darien safely at home. The trip alone was taxing on her physically and she needs much rest. I hope she will be strong enough to carry her baby to full term."

"Son, I'm sorry you have to do this the way it has come about, but I have faith in you. By God's grace you will be successful and Serenity's baby will be healthy and strong and won't come early. Here, take these herbs; they will help. They are safe for her to take. They will enable her to become stronger. And, Son! Don't be alarmed if it appears that she grows weaker in the beginning. That won't last. She will get stronger after her body adjusts to the dosage. Please make sure she is aware of this and knows it will not harm either of them."

"Yes, Father, I shall do as you ask. But before we part, I have to share with you that I have fallen in love with Adriena. Yes, Serenity's sister. I know there isn't much time to talk now, but we hope to be married soon. "

"How wonderful! I have always had a good impression of those sisters and am so happy for you both. You're right, no more talking now. But I'm so very happy that you shared this news with me. Now, Son, you should take every bit of what you need, and hurry. Be sure to keep a watchful eye on Serenity. I, on the other hand, will be returning to Tomáš and his unit. Remember I love you, Son, and take care of my future daughter-in-law. I hope to one day see your happiness come to light. Oh, and, Son, I want you to know you make me very proud to be your father."

He hugged his son as Trevian said, "Please be careful. I hope to see you again, and soon."

Trevian made his way to the clinic rooms and gathered medical supplies, herbs, smelling salts, and birthing supplies, and then made his way to the Bonnaires' residence.

As the first light of dawn's sun spread over the tree-studded meadow and reached into the tent holding the sleeping husband and wife, a strong wind blew the tent flap open, waking the slumbering pair. The sounds of a hundred men breaking camp crept menacingly into the privacy behind the green flaps, bringing the pair to their feet. A long look passed between them, a gnawing feeling of what could have been and a hope of what they might yet still have. Arabel, straightening her hair after throwing her outer clothes over her head and buttoning up, gratefully extended her hand for the cup of coffee and hard roll Tomáš brought to her. Dinner had worn off and the road home would start soon enough. They shared a long goodbye kiss and an embrace that transmitted the electricity of the tie that bound them to each other.

"Arabel, since it isn't safe for you to travel alone, one of my men will accompany you to Markis's house. Do not worry, he will return to me as soon as you are safely there."

She nodded and reached for the reins of the saddled horse. The soldier next to her was young and offered a timid smile, recognizing her position as his commanding officer's wife. One long last look passed between Arabel and Tomáš, and then she turned the horse and they galloped away. Tomáš instructed a few men to return to their stronghold on the battlefield with instructions to bring Trevian's father, Barron Strombalini, back to the group for their march on the enemy.

The meadow fell behind the galloping horses and the woods drew near once again. The path was worn and easy to follow, which was not necessarily a good thing in times of war. Clouds had been gathering, bringing a cool shade to the riders in the woods, who seemed to be engrossed in their own thoughts, the younger rider alert to their surroundings, the woman deep in thought about love and life and its twists and turns. How wonderful it was to be with Tomáš once again. It was as if they had never aged. There was passion and tenderness. The beating of his heart upon hers. The smell of his manliness and how he had continued to hold her even as he thought her asleep.

212

With his hand up in the air, her soldier companion signaled for them to slow cautiously as they came up to a split in the trail. They stopped.

Yes, there were sounds of another traveler coming their way. Was it a friend or a foe? Then, through the thinning branches of the trees, Arabel recognized the rider. It was Trevian! He was as surprised as she, and pulled in his horse, laying his hand on his hat.

"Arabel, I'm surprised to see you. Where are you going, and who is this soldier with you?"

"Trevian, I'm on my way to Markis's house. I'll be staying with him until this war is over. This soldier was sent to protect me on this journey. But now that you are here, he can return to his platoon and report to Tomáš, his commanding officer, that I was delivered safe into your hands."

With that the young soldier took his leave and returned to report to his commanding officer.

When they arrived, Markis opened his door to welcome Trevian and Arabel. He said to Trevian, "It is a good thing you showed up. I was about to come look for you."

"Sorry, sir, I was detained and I have something that will help Serenity. My father recommended it, so if you would excuse me, I would like to get this to her immediately."

"Sure, son, go ahead. One of my men will help you get to where they are."

Trevian hurried, following Alaster down the trail and into the caverns to their location.

Markis said to Arabel, "It is good to see you. And what brings you to my home? Last I heard, you were going to meet Tomáš and then back to your home."

"Yes, Markis, I did say that. I had a long talk with Tomáš about your offer to stay here along with the girls. He said to tell you he will allow this for our daughters' sake. He also said to tell you he appreciates your hospitality and all that you are doing and have done for our family. Markis, I can sense a change in him. I can tell he is already fighting it, only this time I fear that it is truly worse."

"Arabel, you know I will do anything I can to help him. I, too, know how stubborn he is. I've sent some of the men under my command to keep an eye on him. They are to help him if he is in need of them. He is not aware of this and I would like it to remain that way. Do you need to pick anything up at your house?"

"Markis, yes, I need some things, and I do appreciate the kindness you have given to my whole family."

"Very well, I will have an escort for you in the morning. Arabel, you mean a lot to me, as does your family. You know my feelings have never changed, but I do respect Tomáš. Would you like to see your daughters?"

"Yes, of course I would."

"Arabel, I cannot let you see the path, so I will have to cover your eyes and lead you there. Forgive me, but it is only to take precautions for now. It needs to be your daughters' decision. Will you please do this?"

"Yes, of course—anything, as long as I can see them. I want to see our grandchild as much as you do, and I hope that Serenity is doing well. I truly accept the hospitality and I will do as you ask. I want my girls to know they can trust me, and I also need to tell them what their father said."

"Arabel, as you have just seen, Trevian has already gone ahead. Let's give him a little while to check on Serenity. She had a very stressful trip back."

"Is my daughter okay? Is the baby okay?"

"Yes, Arabel, she and the baby will be fine. She will need complete rest and where she is will help her recover. I'll take you to see her in about two hours. Oh, let's have a cup of tea. You look really tired. But before we get onto other subjects, I must tell you, Adriena is engaged to Trevian. The only reason I tell is so that you don't become upset if you see them close together. Please let her come to tell you, and don't give away that I mentioned it to you."

"Oh my, Markis! When did this all come about?"

"She will have to tell you, but I believe it happened while they were traveling through the caverns on their way to the detention camp with Serenity."

"I will not say a word, Markis, and I will listen. My babies are all grown up. If there's one thing I've learned from them, it is patience. Something Tomáš has a hard time with."

Markis laughed at the memory of his friend and his patience, or lack of it. "How well do I remember!"

Arabel laughed at his remark.

Trevian finally reached Adriena and told her he needed to do a thorough exam on Serenity. He said, "I brought special herbs my father told me to give her. This will make her stronger, but in the beginning it will make her rest a good bit until her body's strength is built up." As he gave her a quick kiss he said, "I will be back in a little bit to have your full attention. Damn, you're beautiful, and I've missed you."

He quickly kissed her again and she took him to her sister, smiling as she said, "I've missed you too, and I was so worried about you!"

Trevian examined Serenity, telling her about the herbs his father had suggested so she could start taking them. She agreed without question.

Darien, who had been watching, now stepped out of the room with Trevian to hear the prognosis. "Make sure she follows these instructions and does as little as possible. Right now she needs lots of rest. To ease your mind, she and the baby seem to be fine. She just needs to rest and regain her strength."

Trevian left Darien with Serenity while he walked back to Adriena to explain what had happened to him.

Finally alone, if only for an hour or so, Darien looked upon Serenity's face, remembering what he'd left behind. Intensely, he held her and said, "Never will I ever leave your side." He leaned in and kissed her.

Not wanting to lose the moment, Serenity replied in a whisper, his eyes upon her face, "I still can't believe you are here. Please tell me this is not a dream?"

As he leaned in to kiss her again in between each breath, brushing her lips with his, he said, "Does this feel like a dream?"

She kissed him back, smiling, then said with a kiss, "No, never." Throwing her arms around him to hold him close, she said, "I'm never letting you out of my sight again."

He pulled away slightly and lightly tapped her nose with his finger to say, "You need to rest for our son or daughter to come."

She pulled him close and said, "Stay with me. Don't leave."

"I will stay as long as you want me to. Close your eyes and rest a bit." With that he released the clasps on the curtains and created a cozy private space, hiding them within the cocoon of the giant king-size bed.

She snuggled close, laying her head on his shoulder just as she fell asleep. Darien caressed her forehead lightly while pressing his lips on it.

Chapter 32

Acceptance

The tea did its job and the English crumpets filled with cheese and chopped ham were just the right amount for Arabel. Breakfast had just been the cup of coffee and hard roll with Tomáš. Her face softened as she remembered.

Sitting and talking about old times, when Markis's son and Arabel's girls were youngsters, melted the minutes and hours away. Then, as promised, Markis took Arabel to the hiding place. The journey through the caverns wasn't easy for the blindfolded Arabel. She held tightly to Markis's hand, stumbling only a few times and using it to steady herself.

Markis removed the blindfold from her eyes and said, "Wait here, just for a moment. I need to tell them you are here and see if I can get them to let you come and go as needed. Arabel, this place is not to be shared with anyone outside. Can you do this? One more thing: Tomáš is not to know this for any reason. Please understand that the state of mind he is in may jeopardize this whole area. I worked many years to build this hiding place and add what is needed in the event that the war continued to worsen. Please, I need you to do this, so they can stay safe."

"Yes, Markis, I will and can do this. I, too, want what's best for them."

"Very good. Wait here. I'll be back in a little bit."

Arabel walked to a nearby chair, took a seat, and studied the hanging tapestry on the adjoining wall. What a beautiful and skillfully made piece of art it was! She immediately recognized its value and marveled that this kind of finery could be found in a "cave." Equally interesting were the rows and rows of ceiling-height bookcases lining the walls. What beautifully bound books! Arabel hadn't seen books of such quality or number since she had left the "old" country before the last war. Yet here was history and literature…the best literature, and looking closer, she found most of the most famous authors.

Trevian looked at Adriena and said, "Your father stopped and talked to me before I left you in the detention cavern. He also sent an escort with me to my father's house. When I got there, I told him that Tomáš wanted him to come quickly."

Adriena said, "How is Father, Trevian?"

"He was nice to me. He told me to say hello to his daughters for him. Truth be told, I was in a hurry to see you again." He pulled her close into a warm embrace with a hint of a smile. Slowly, he kissed her with a deep affection, holding her firmly in place. In between his kisses he said, "Every minute I'm away from you is too long."

He pulled away to say, "I met your mother on the way to Markis's home. She is there and I think he is going to bring her here. I don't know that for sure. I just wanted to make you aware she is here. You know as well as I know how Markis is and I wouldn't put it past him bringing her here."

"Thank you for telling me. Part of me says to let her come and the other says I wish she wouldn't. I'm just so confused sometimes."

"If this makes you feel at all at ease, she did tell me on the way here that she spoke to your father."

"Do you know what she said? Please tell me, I need to know!"

"Adriena, calm down. She told me this, that she just saved Darien's life because of Serenity."

"Trevian, did she say at all how?"

"No, I'm sorry. That is all she would tell me. I did not want to tell you this; I can tell your father is getting worse. The sickness he has, the madness grows within him. It is only a matter of time before this happens, but when that will be, I do not know."

"Wait a minute! What? What madness? What are you talking about?"

"You didn't know any of this?"

"No! Trevian, this is the first I've heard of it."

"Adriena, my father has been by his side most of the time and he sees the changes in him. They are the same as the last war. My father and Markis witnessed it firsthand."

"No, Trevian, I knew none of this! If my mother knew, I wonder why she did not tell us any of. This…this…" Her voice cracked as she tried to speak through her tears. "This explains his bitterness toward us. I need to talk to my mother."

Trevian pulled her close, letting her tears flow at will. "Don't worry, my love, you will." Changing the subject, he said, as he lifted her chin so that her eyes met his, "I just remembered. We still have a wedding to plan, do we or do we not?"

He smiled at her, finally bringing a smile to her face, and she said, "Yes, of course we do. My feelings are still the same."

Trevian looked at her to say, "When do you think will be a good time? What are your thoughts on this?"

"I would like to be there for my sister until the baby is here. Though I want to marry now, I need to focus on Serenity and help her be strong. Our connection is deep and I don't want to be away from her at all. It's a twin thing and hard to explain, I hope you can understand. It does not change my feelings for you in the least. Can you help me through this first?"

"Honey, I will wait for you as long as it takes. Besides, I'm not going anywhere, we have to deliver this baby!" He leaned toward her and kissed her worries away.

It was at this point that Markis stepped into the room. "Am I interrupting?" He addressed the startled couple. "I wanted to tell you that I have brought Arabel here to see you and Serenity. I'm hoping that you will both agree to put aside any grievances and come together. Your mother loves you and Serenity so very much. It has been very difficult for her these last months, especially after your father was called back to the war effort."

"Markis, I think that Serenity and I will both be happy to be reconciled with Mother. We know that she has been torn between following Father's rules and wanting the best for us. But let us talk about it together. Trevian and I will come with you now. Serenity is sleeping and can join us later."

It was evening now, but within the cave there wasn't a sun to track for time. Only the growling of Trevian's stomach as he and Adriena followed Markis to the library room, where Arabel was waiting, alerted them that dinnertime was fast approaching. As they walked, Adriena's thoughts tumbled in her mind. What would happen now? Should they allow Mother to come and go? Should Mother stay here with them? What would be the timing for her marriage; could she really wait until after the birth of her niece or nephew? So many unanswered questions, one right after the other. Adriena consciously pushed them from her mind for the moment as she heard the dinner call from Michiko.

Adriena suddenly heard a noise coming from Serenity's room. She ran to see what was going on. "Oh my God Serenity!" Adriena calls for Trevian come quick. "Serenity is hemorrhaging."

Serenity screams "Help me!" as she passes out.

About the Author

Leanna was born and raised in South Georgia. She started writing at a very young age due to traumatic experiences. She enjoys time spent in the mountains, and traveling with family and friends. The heartfelt passions experienced in her writings are drawn from personal experiences and an incredibly vivid imagination. Readers should be advised that reading any of Leanna's romance and adventure romance novels will start an endearing relationship with the author herself.

Books By Author Leanna Sellers

Poetry

A Vision Inspired By The Heart (2013)
Inward Ties (2016)
Shadows Of The Heart (2018)
Unbreakable Bonds (2018)
Pillars Of The Earth (2021)

Novels

Awaken The Fury (2013)

(Through the Eyes of Serenity Series)
Through the Eyes of Serenity, Book 1

Leanna's books are available on Amazon.com in Kindle and
paperback formats at: https://www.amazon.com/-/e/B00J0BPTTC